THE AMAZING DYLAN ALCOTT

WELBECK

Published in 2022 by Welbeck Publishing Pty Ltd,
part of Welbeck Publishing Group,

Offices in:
London - 20 Mortimer Street, London W1T 3JW
Sydney - 205 Commonwealth Street, Surry Hills 2010

www.welbeckpublishing.com

ISBN: 9781922853011

Welbeck acknowledges the Traditional Owners and Custodians of this land and gives respect to the Elders – past and present – and through them to all Australian Aboriginal and Torres Strait Islander people.

Printed and bound in Australia by McPherson's Printing Group

10 9 8 7 6 5 4 3 2 1

A catalogue record for this book is available from the National Library of Australia

Statistics and records correct as of August 2022

The paper in this book is FSC® certified.
FSC® promotes environmentally responsible, socially beneficial and economically viable management of the world's forests.

THE AMAZING DYLAN ALCOTT

Chris Maher

Illustrated by
Jules Faber

WELBECK

CONTENTS

CHAPTER ONE

AUSTRALIAN OF THE YEAR

Every Australia Day, one person is chosen to represent the country for a whole year.

This person must have qualities that are important to Australians – that sum up what it means to be Australian. They must have strengths that inspire us all. That make people across the country say, ***this is the sort of person I want to be!***

Australians of the Year have been famous artists, musicians, novelists, dancers, politicians, advocates, priests, entrepreneurs, community leaders, doctors, philanthropists, soldiers and scientists.

There have been famous athletes, swimmers, sailors, boxers, cricketers, runners, tennis players and footballers.

But never a Paralympian.

Never a disabled athlete.

This country had never seen their most celebrated person as someone who was in a wheelchair.

Yet!

Each State selects a nominee for The Australian of the Year.

In 2022, the nominee from South Australia was a doctor who helped saved thousands of lives through her vaccine research.

The Northern Territory nominee saved Indigenous people from unfairly going to prison.

The Tasmanian nominee helped save the world's oceans from plastic pollution, and saved thousands of marine animals in the process.

The ACT nominee was a philanthropist who fought racial injustice – and was also a successful Olympian and NBA basketball player.

The New South Wales nominee invented a way to turn waste into steel, helping save the environment and the economy.

The Queensland nominee fought to stop family violence.

The Western Australian nominee helped homeless people and young people in trouble.

But imagine if somehow YOU are the 2022 Victorian nominee...

And you're not an amazing researcher or inventor, you didn't keep people from jail or save the world's oceans – you are someone who describes yourself as just hitting tennis balls for a living!!!

And – unlike all the other nominees – you are in a wheelchair.

Imagine how nervous you'd be.

All these eminent people have been nominated. And you are here amongst them.

You've had successes. But no disabled person has **EVER** been made Australian of the Year.

It seems impossible...

But.

BUT!

You notice something as you wheel into the venue.

Whoever wins, they will have to go up onto the stage. There is a set of small steps at the front of the stage, where you would expect the winner to walk up to collect their award and make a short acceptance speech.

But to the side of the stage, there is a ramp. Why would the stage have a ramp leading up to it?

Maybe because the winner can't walk up the stairs?

Maybe because the winner is in a wheelchair!

You hold your breath.

Is this possible?

After all these years, when no Australian leader was ever in a wheelchair.

You've never even seen a person with disabilities on TV or in the newspapers unless it was a story about their disability or unless it was some sort of tragedy.

No one in a wheelchair has ever been celebrated as someone to look up to.

Would people all over the country aspire to be like **YOU?**

The Prime Minister, Scott Morrison, stands on the stage, ready to announce the winner.

"The 2022 Australian of the Year is…"

Everyone holds their collective breath, waiting for the winner.

And you hear your name called out!!

The audience erupts in applause. You take off your covid mask and wheel yourself up to the stage. Up the ramp! That ***IS*** why the ramp was there!

Your girlfriend gives you a big kiss. She is so emotional and proud. She seems to be crying.

IT'S UNBELIEVABLE

One person out of all the Australians to choose from. And they chose **YOU**.

And the best thing: when you were growing up, people with disabilities were never held up as role models.

And now a person with a disability – a person like you – is being celebrated on stage as someone to take inspiration from.

WHAT A GIANT LEAP. WHAT AN AMAZING ACCOMPLISHMENT!

For you, it's an Australian dream starting to come true – imagine a country where people with disabilities are respected for their abilities, and not underestimated because of their disabilities.

But how did this all come about?

How did you – just a kid in a wheelchair – become so respected that you were chosen to be Australian of the Year?

How did that kid in a wheelchair become a **Golden Slam** winner, a four-time **Gold Paralympian** with fifteen singles titles, someone who organises music festivals, is a radio presenter, has their own charitable foundation and runs an employment agency for disabled people?

How did that kid become someone who never stops trying to change the world's idea of what people with disabilities can achieve – and who uses their profile as a successful sportsperson to do it.

YOU are an unbelievably hard trainer and worker.

A fighter who inspires others to do their best – to do better than they ever thought possible...

TO DO BETTER THAN *OTHER PEOPLE* THOUGHT THEY COULD DO.

Everyone in the audience stands and claps as you make your way to the microphone. You fight to hold back tears, but that doesn't stop you making a joke:

"I think standing ovations are the most ironic things in the world by the way! But I'll take them!"

Everyone laughs.

"It's a huge honour!"

The tears change from tears of joy to tears of sadness as you remember how much you used to hate having a disability. And how you never saw anyone like you on TV. But now you know how lucky you are to have the best family, and partner and team.

Because now you are proud of the person you are and the amazing life you've lived.

It's quite a story...

It's the story of Dylan Alcott, Australian of the Year.

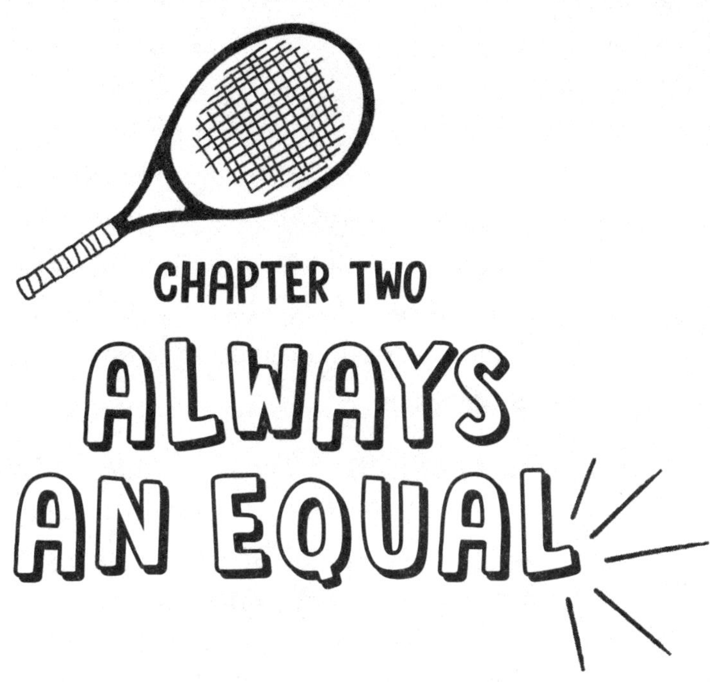

CHAPTER TWO
ALWAYS AN EQUAL

This story begins on 4 December 1990, when Dylan Alcott was born in the Melbourne suburb of Sandringham.

An early Christmas present, he seemed big and healthy at first. But there was something that worried the doctors – a large lump on his back. In the beginning, they thought it was nothing to worry about – but once they did some tests, they got very concerned.

It was a tumour wrapped around his spine.

Every time little Dylan moved, the tumour moved his spinal column and the baby would scream in agony. Everyone was very worried, but the doctors couldn't operate on so small a baby. They had to wait until he was at least five weeks old to be strong enough to handle such a serious operation.

The doctors told Dylan's parents they could take him home. They weren't sure he was going to live, so they thought at least that way the family would all have one Christmas together.

After Christmas, when they decided he was strong enough, he was readied for surgery. The surgeon, Miss Lewis, said she would do her best, but it might not be enough. He might die during the operation.

Imagine how worried and sad his parents and his brother Zack were.

Their little baby was in danger. They didn't know if he'd survive.

He did survive.

But it wasn't long before he had complications from the operation, and nearly died a second time. Again, he came through, to everyone's enormous relief.

The surgeon told his parents they didn't have to worry anymore.

And he certainly had to fight.

He went through several medical procedures in the first three years of his life. One of them meant he had to lie on his stomach for three months without moving!

How hard would that be for a child or an adult, let alone a little baby?

Dylan had thirteen operations over this time, and several times his little life was in danger.

At three years of age, Dylan finally came home to live. He had limited mobility in his legs, but he was able to get around with the help of a tiny pair of crutches.

It was clear little Dylan wasn't the same as his brother. But his parents made a decision that would help Dylan in the long run.

Whenever possible, they treated Dylan and Zack the same.

They were determined that their little boy would be a full member of the family, treated the same as everyone. And that he would have the same opportunities to enjoy life and succeed in it.

He would be an equal.

Not be defined by his disability.

They made changes around the house to make it easier for little Dylan to get around, such as installing a lift so his bedroom could be upstairs like everyone else's.

His mum made sure he could get out and be physical and took him to the local pool where he learned to swim.

Dylan took to the freedom of the water like a fish. All the time his upper body, hands and arms were getting stronger, making up for the lack of mobility in his legs.

They improvised ways for him to get around, like his little crutches, a skateboard, and even a stroller when they went to the shops. But after a little girl looked into the stroller expecting to find a baby and saw him instead, Dylan said that was enough.

So at four years old, he got his first wheelchair.

And with a wheelchair – once he got the hang of it – came freedom.

But being treated as an equal can be hard. For example, at home he still crawled on the carpet to get around. And this left his brother with a big advantage.

Siblings love to jostle for anything they have to share. It's just natural. Number one on the Alcott boys' list of precious items was the TV remote control.

While Zack held the remote out of reach of his brother, little Dylan would use his superior arm strength to hang on indefinitely. But being able to stand upright, Zack could simply put it on top of the fridge.

At the time this really annoyed Dylan but as he grew up, he realised he was being treated exactly as Zack would treat him if he didn't have a disability – getting whatever advantage he could to secure the remote.

He was treating him as an equal, and that helped Dylan work his way around problems, and made him stronger for later life.

Even at a young age Dylan was interested in all sorts of sports.

He loved Aussie rules. His family was very sporty, and some of the Carlton players were friends of their family. He even "managed" his brother's Aussie rules team, with the help of his dad.

Dylan loved cricket – his uncle was the Australian team's physiotherapist, Errol Alcott, and they got to meet some of the Test players.

In the neighbourhood cricket games, Dylan played in his wheelchair, making it very hard for anyone to bowl him out. He couldn't get out Leg Before Wicket in his chair, and there was no such rule as Wheelchair Before Wicket!

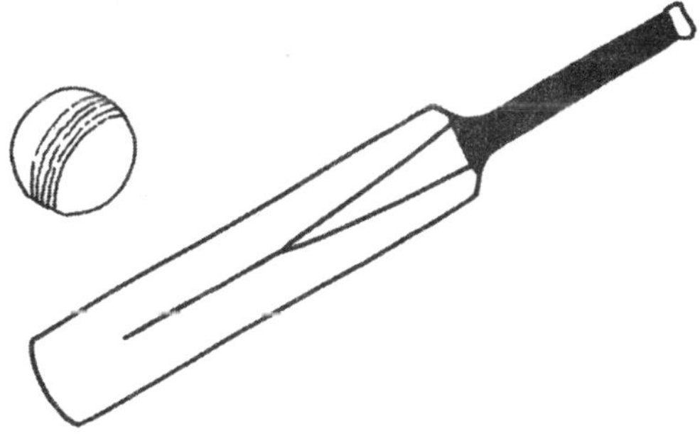

He played basketball in casual games with the kids who lived on his dead-end street, ideal for neighbourhood games.

He also loved tennis and even had a poster of Pat Rafter, Australia's Wimbledon champion, on his wall.

And both he and his brother loved skateboarding. They named their cat Chad after skater Chad Muska. They wanted a dog to start with, but dogs kept knocking Dylan over when he was little, so they settled for a cat.

They loved Chad and he was a great calming influence and friend for Dylan. (And Chad becomes very important later in the story.)

Dylan and Zack both went to Saint Joan of Arc school in Brighton. There, ***Dylan even competed in running races*** – using his new aluminium crutches and starting on the halfway line.

But of all the sports he loved, swimming was the first one he really excelled at.

Swimming can be a great activity for people with disabilities – especially if they have mobility issues. The water holds them up and they can experience a freedom they just can't achieve on dry land.

Even adults with disabilities can get great benefits from exercising or just floating the water, as there is less pressure on their joints and bodies than on land.

With Dylan's upper body and arm strength from using the wheelchair, **HE SMASHED IT!**

He swam against kids without disabilities – **AND STILL WON!**

He was picked to represent his school in backstroke, butterfly and freestyle.

About this time he also learned about Louise Sauvage. She was the first Australian athlete with a disability to have a big profile. She won nine gold and four silver Paralympic medals as well as eleven gold and two silver World Championship medals. On top of that she won four Boston Marathons.

The sight of her tearing down the road on her three-wheeled racing wheelchair was beamed around the world, and she became the face of the Paralympics, especially for Australians.

Like Dylan, Louise had been born with a severe spinal condition which gave her only limited control over her legs, and she also had scoliosis, which makes her spine curve.

Despite her disabilities she succeeded in sport.

SHE WAS A CHAMPION!

The best in the world!

Dylan was inspired. Maybe he could be a champion too?

Success was coming in swimming, so for a while his dream was to become a Paralympic swimmer. He trained three times a week, putting all his effort into it.

Then he heard about a triathlon for kids that was going to be held at Port Melbourne Beach called the Weetbix Kids Tryathalon. More than a thousand able-bodied kids were competing, including some friends from school.

He wanted to compete too!

Of course, being in a wheelchair was going to make it a bit tricky, but his family was determined to let him compete the same way as other kids could.

It was a "fun event", with no prizes or places, so the organisers were happy to allow Dylan to have his dad help out.

His dad kept an eye on him in the swimming leg, just to be sure he'd be okay. He and Dylan did the cycling leg together on a tandem bike (with Dylan just pretending to peddle). Then Dylan pushed his wheelchair home on the 500-metre run to the finish line.

There was a large crowd there, and they were all cheering Dylan home.

He couldn't get the smile off his face.

HE'D DONE IT!

Dylan had competed with a thousand kids from around Victoria. And he'd finished the race, even if he'd had a little help.

A photographer took a picture of him and it appeared in the Sunday newspaper.

That was something to remember.

More than that, it was something to spur him on to greater things.

CHAPTER THREE
TOUGH TIMES

When Dylan was in entering his final year of primary school, he was offered a scholarship to attend a large – and expensive – private school called Brighton Grammar.

The scholarship was set up by the parents of a student, Mark Comport, who tragically died when he was in Year 6. They wanted to help other boys with a disability who couldn't afford to go to the school.

Dylan was the first person to get the scholarship.

He knew he was lucky and really appreciated the opportunity. He enjoyed the sports, music and school lessons on offer. He got a good education and in particular loved public speaking and debating. This would come in very handy later in his life, when he had to talk to famous people, address large audiences and appear on television and radio.

But while he appreciated the opportunities, ***not everything was good***.

After he had been at the school a little while, bullies started targeting him.

This became a hard time for Dylan. A **very** hard time.

Being bullied is always unpleasant. Bullies try to find a weakness they can tease you about. They want you to feel bad about yourself.

Sometimes they do it to make themselves feel big in front of other kids. But for the person being teased, it can be devastating.

There's the old saying: sticks and stones can break your bones but names will never hurt you.

That's easy to say, but in the heat of the moment, when bullies are calling you names and saying horrible things about you, trying to make you feel bad about yourself, it can be hard to ignore.

Having a visible disability can make you a special target for bullies, because they can immediately bully you about it. If you're in a wheelchair or have to walk with crutches, bullies might think that's funny. It's certainly not funny to the person being bullied.

They've done nothing to deserve it, but the bullies are making their lives a misery.

That's when you can start to doubt yourself. Start to think those horrible things they say are true. If you let it, it can make you weaker. And that's what the bullies want – to prove they have the power to make someone weak.

You can fight against them, but it isn't easy.

It's even harder for disabled people getting bullied, because they don't often see other disabled people on TV or the movies. And they never see them winning.

At least, that was mostly the case when Dylan was young, although it is getting a little bit better now.

And the bullying, combined with the image of disabled people being losers, made Dylan feel very isolated.

Later, he wished he'd spoken to someone about it, but at the time he kept it all to himself, and he suffered because of it.

In reality, you don't have to deal with things like that by yourself, you can talk to people who care about you, and they can help. But sometimes when you're being bullied you forget that, or feel embarrassed or scared to talk about it. But talking about it does help. It can make it better.

But Dylan didn't talk about it with anyone. He went further into himself, staying home and eating junk food. He started to get overweight, unhealthy and very unhappy.

There were two things that helped him. Music was one. Sport was the other.

He loved playing games at school and with his friends, but as the other able-bodied boys his age got bigger and stronger, Dylan found it harder to compete against them.

But when he was competing against other boys his age who had a disability – he smashed it!

One day, Dylan went to an event organised by Wheelchair Sports Victoria where kids could try wheelchair tennis.

THIS WAS A TURNING POINT IN DYLAN'S LIFE.

First, because he tried wheelchair tennis and loved it!

And also because he met his long-time friend and doubles partner, Heath Davidson.

Heath contracted a virus in his spine when he was only five months old, so like Dylan he had been in a wheelchair his whole life. He was more than three years older than Dylan, but they became great friends, based on their mutual love of tennis.

Although it was becoming hard for Dylan to compete against able-bodied players, **he practised against them**, and that honed his skills and improved his resilience.

Both Heath and Dylan were overweight, but the more they trained the fitter they got, and the faster they managed to move their wheelchairs around the court.

Unfortunately, just as he was getting into the swing of tennis, he had a setback.

A VERY BIG SETBACK

He needed another operation on his back. It was a nine hour operation and unfortunately while he was being operated on, the doctors damaged his bladder, meaning he had to stay in hospital for two months, lying on his stomach the whole time.

Imagine how uncomfortable, and how boring that would be for even a single day.

But for two months!

All told, it took him six months without moving to recover. All that time not moving meant his legs wasted away and he lost the little bit of mobility he had in them.

From then on, there would be no more crutches.

He would need a wheelchair to get around, all the time.

That could be very disheartening.

But Dylan didn't let it get him down.

Once he had fully recovered, he worked on getting fit again.

He threw himself into wheelchair tennis. Training hard, building up his strength, and developing his skills.

And he was rewarded!

Dylan was chosen to play in the 2001 Junior National Disabled Games.

He was chosen not only to play in tennis, but also the first sport he was successful in – swimming.

Dylan was representing Victoria, and kids from every state in the country were there. Most of them were older than him but somehow, he beat them all in the 50-metre butterfly race!

Not only did he win the race,

HE BROKE THE AUSTRALIAN RECORD!

A record that still stands today.

He also came second in the breaststroke and backstroke.

And in a sign of things to come – **he got a bronze in the doubles tennis**.

This led to bigger things in the world of tennis, and he was chosen to play in the under-18 boys Australian Wheelchair Open.

He made the finals in the singles.

Better still, he played doubles with his mate Heath, and they won!

He and Heath were now champions!

Although Heath was fourteen, Dylan was only eleven – and he was the under-18 doubles champion!

AMAZING, FOR A KID WHO HAD BEEN DOUBTING HIMSELF.

Now, at a tender age, he had a sport he could sink his teeth into. Something he knew he was good at. Something that was keeping him fit and making him happy.

And he had a friend who liked the same things, and was in a similar situation.

Things were looking up.

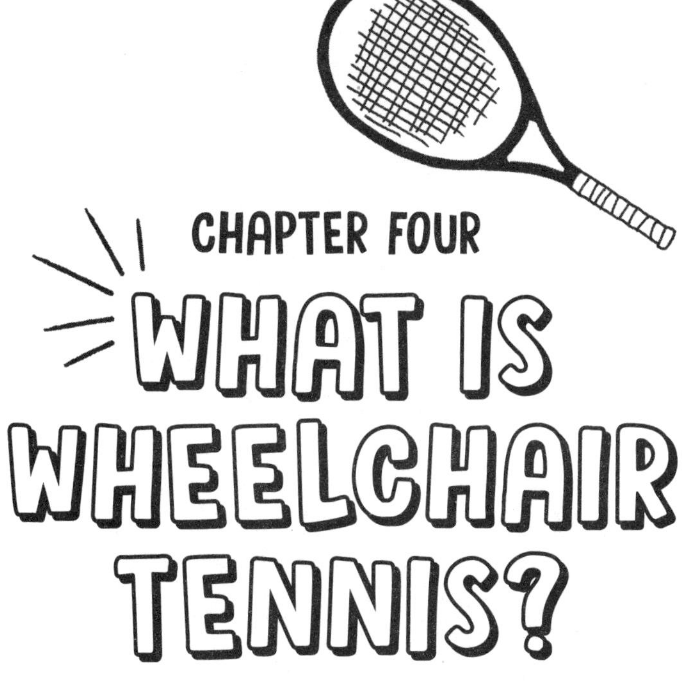

CHAPTER FOUR

WHAT IS WHEELCHAIR TENNIS?

Most people know what tennis is, and know about the stars of the game like Roger Federer, Rafael Nadal, Novak Djokovic, Ash Barty and Venus and Serena Williams.

But what is wheelchair tennis? Is it the same as able-bodied tennis, just played in wheelchairs? How did it start? Who thought up the rules? And who can qualify to play in tournaments and the Paralympics?

It all started back in 1976 when a young American man had a skiing accident. Brad Parks was eighteen years old and a fantastic skier. He wanted to turn professional one day and have a career as a freestyle skier.

He was competing in an event in Utah, USA, scooting down a snow covered slope. He took off and spun in the air, but as he came down, he landed incorrectly on hard ice.

The accident left him paralysed from the hips down. He would need a wheelchair for the rest of his life.

Brad was a serious athlete and he didn't want to stop being one, even though he now had a disability.

He wasn't going to let the disability bring him down – in fact, it spurred him onto bigger things.

As part of his rehabilitation, he started playing wheelchair basketball. He got very good at moving his chair around the court. He wondered if he could play tennis in a wheelchair, so he got his father to hit some tennis balls to him. He liked it, but his chair was very hard to manoeuvre.

Brad checked in at Rancho Los Amigos rehabilitation centre in California, where they had a new recreational therapist who was himself in a wheelchair. His name was Jeff Minnebraker, and he'd been injured in a car accident.

Jeff wasn't in any old wheelchair.

He had developed his own super lightweight, ultra-manoeuvrable wheelchair. Jeff described it as the ***sports car of wheelchairs***. He'd also removed the push handles from the back of the wheelchair. He didn't want anyone to push him around – he was going to do it all himself!

When you saw Jeff in his chair, you just saw him and a set of wheels. No armrests, no push handles. It was like they had become the one being.

Brad wanted a chair just like it, and asked Jeff to make him one.

Jeff refused. But he told Brad:

Jeff was getting the patients to play wheelchair tennis as part of their rehab. And it was working.

It made them fitter, and it was a lot of fun. It added an exciting, positive and healthy element to their rehabilitation.

Because the new chairs were life-changing, Brad, Jeff and some of the other wheelchair tennis players started making and selling them under the brand name Quadra.

Before long, wheelchair tennis had caught the interest of lots of people in wheelchairs who wanted to play sport.

By the 1980s it became very popular and a national 10-tournament circuit was developed throughout the United States, with a big national championship finishing off the season.

Although Jeff was the genius behind the chairs, Brad used his business know-how to attract attention and make them more popular. He was helped by Randy Snow, another wheelchair tennis player who had become disabled after a farm accident in Texas.

The big breakthrough came when wheelchair tennis became a full-medal sport at the Paralympic Games in Barcelona in 1992.

Brad and Randy played and won the first men's doubles gold medal!

The World Team Cup was also set up. It was like tennis' Davis Cup, where players represented their countries in an international competition. Over the years, it has been contested by 52 different nations.

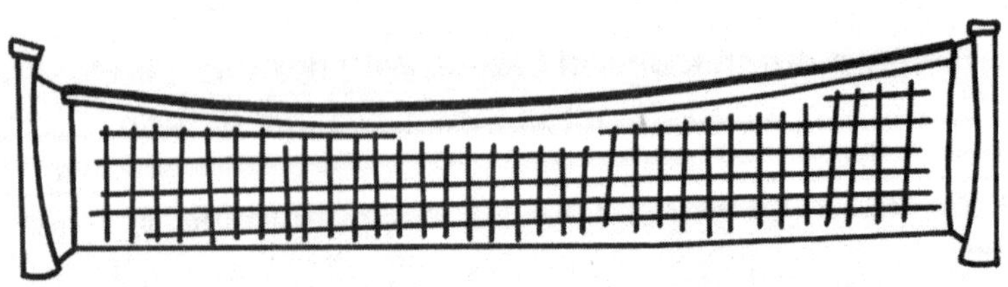

What is different about wheelchair tennis?

For a start, everyone plays in a wheelchair. But what else?

Foot faults don't apply for obvious reasons, so they have wheel faults instead. Also, in the Quad division, men and women can compete against each other. Sometimes players with hand disabilities have the racquet taped to their hand or arm.

Most other rules are the same, except for the main difference: ***the ball can bounce twice before you have to return it back over the net***.

One of those bounces **must** be inside the court – but the second one can be outside and you still have a chance to get the ball back – if you can get to it. Of course, you can always still hit it on the full – volley it – or hit it after the first bounce if you like.

The reason for the second bounce rule is that someone in a wheelchair can't get to the ball as quickly as a person running, so they need the extra time to make up the distance.

Some wheelchair athletes can zoom along at 30 kmh when racing...

But on a tennis court it is hard to build up that sort of speed, while still being able to manoeuvre and change direction quickly. In fact, one of the most important skills to succeed at wheelchair tennis is mobility. Being able to turn quickly to get where the ball is going fast. Of course, anticipation is important, so you need to know where to go. But the skill and strength needed to turn and get on the move is probably the most valuable ability in wheelchair tennis.

CHAPTER FIVE

NEVER STOP MOVING

Mobility on the court is so important in wheelchair tennis that ***good players never stop***.

They are on the move the whole time. Once you stop dead still, it's hard to get going fast enough to reach the ball, and you can easily be caught out.

Watching Dylan play wheelchair tennis is like watching a ***shark patrolling a patch of water***, waiting to strike. He never stops. He moves in

quick circles and then pounces, zooming to where he needs to be, giving himself plenty of time to line up the perfect shot.

After playing a shot, players sometimes wheel into the doubles alley (also called the tramlines) and turn around, facing the width of the court, so they can head to a safe position where they can return the next ball.

Sometimes they turn their back to the net, their opponent and the ball.

They will then roll towards the baseline, checking over their shoulder as they go, trying to be in position by the time the ball comes back their way.

STRATEGY IS IMPORTANT.

Keeping your opponent guessing which way the ball will go is a key tactic in both able-bodied tennis and wheelchair tennis. A strategy using this tactic might be to move your opponent further and further to one side of the court, until changing and sending the ball to down the line, or across court to the other side.

Famous wheelchair tennis coach Jason Harnett said the players have to start **thinking with their hands**. That is, move to where you need to be instinctively.

The muscle memory in your hands takes you where you need to be, when you need to be there.

Wheeling the chair is also quite a skill as you have to learn how to use both hands to move the chair quickly – **even though you are holding a racquet**. Some people push the rims (the extra circle on the outside of the actual wheel) and others push the rims and the tyres at the same time.

There are also particular wheeling techniques you have to learn. One is pushing one wheel forward with one hand, and the other wheel backwards with the other hand. This enables you to spin on the spot, turning around quick smart.

DYLAN IS AN
EXPERT
AT THIS MOVE!

Modern sporting wheelchairs have wheels that are very splayed out with an average 20 degrees of camber (the angle of the wheels). The camber can vary from 16 degrees up to 22 degrees. That helps the chair change direction faster, gives it more stability, and makes it faster over a short distance.

Because of the camber, the tyres wear out on one side, so you can flip them over after a while. The hand rims can be rubber or foam rather than metal, which is specifically good for tennis, so you can hold the racquet against the hand rim to help push without the racquet slipping.

The chairs also have anti-tip wheels so you don't go over leaning back. Wheelchair basketball players get tipped out of their chairs a lot!

And if you've ever watched wheelchair rugby (also called murder ball because it is so tough) you'll see those players get knocked over all the time – but their chairs are reinforced as if they are going into battle!

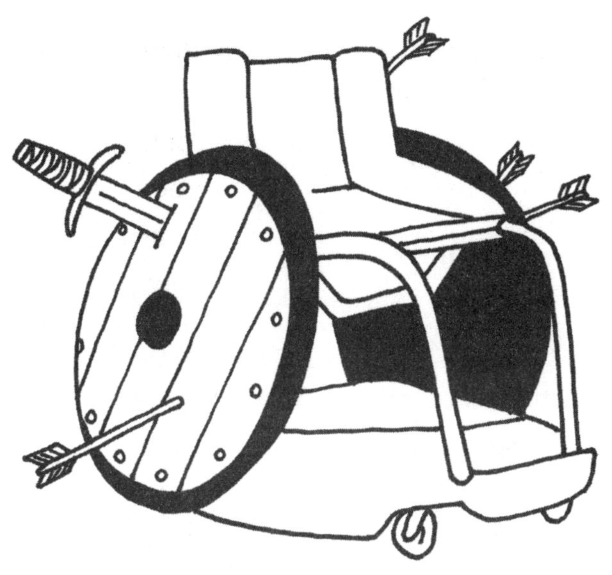

There are toe clips to keep your feet in the chair, as well as straps across your body so your effort to hit the ball doesn't throw you out.

The main thing with pushing is to start hard – two big strong pushes get you going, then it's easy to maintain your momentum. You have to use your shoulders and your core (the muscles around the middle of your body) and keep your head up all the time to see what's happening. If you have a strong core (and some players won't of course, depending on their disability) you can actually turn the chair just by turning your body and moving your hips.

Some drills to help mobility include two players chasing each other around the court, trying to grab the back of each other's chairs. Another is one player holding the other player's chair while they push, helping improve strength for that important first push, and also zig-zagging practice.

Hitting the ball is obviously very important. Most of the basics are the same as standard tennis, but the most important thing is getting the chair in the right position. Often players move into the court to hit the ball, then back out behind the baseline to prepare for the next shot. This means they will move in a V-shaped pattern into and out of the court. You have to make sure the ball is always in front of you.

With backhand shots, to save time, some players use the same grip as for a forehand shot, which is called a reverse backhand. In this move, you hit the ball with the same side of the racquet as a conventional forehand. It looks awkward, but can be effective.

You need to be able to push your chair hard with your non-dominant hand (left hand for right-handed players) and also pull backwards hard too, especially when going for a backhand, to twist your body into the right position.

There are also more subtle moves, such as touching the dominant side wheel with your non-dominant hand to slow one wheel, turning the chair around.

Then there's the question of who can compete against who.

There are two class divisions in wheelchair tennis, Open and Quad.

Open players have a permanent, substantial or total loss of function in one or both legs. They do not however have impaired upper body function.

This includes players with spinal cord injury associated with loss of movement, or serious injuries to one or both hips, knees or ankles, or an amputation.

Quad division have an injury higher up the spine that might impact upper body movement, or a lower body injury plus a functional disability in one or both arms.

Dylan was an Open player originally because he only had a disability to his lower body. But something happened later in life that changed that.

Able-bodied people can also play wheelchair tennis for fun. They just have to get in a chair and abide by the same rules.

CHAPTER SIX

ON A ROLL

Although Dylan was doing well at his studies at school, he was still having trouble with the school social environment.

But competing in wheelchair tennis against other disabled people, he found himself having success.

He was not as fit as he could be – he had been spending too much time eating unhealthy food and feeling isolated. But the more tennis he played, the better he got – the more skills he gained and slowly his fitness improved and started to lose some weight. But he still had a lot further to go.

Wheelchair tennis was something he could focus on, and he put a lot of effort into it.

In January 2004, his tennis practice and effort paid off. He qualified for the National Junior Team in the international wheelchair competition, The World Team Cup, played in New Zealand.

This is like the Davis Cup, but for wheelchair tennis. It is a great achievement to qualify, and a great honour to play.

He was actually representing Australia in international competition!

CAN YOU IMAGINE HOW THAT WOULD FEEL?

He had been doubting himself and feeling bad about his disability. And now he was actually representing his country!

The Australian team played well and nearly won the competition, just losing to The Netherlands – one of the top teams in wheelchair tennis.

And they won the Team of the Year Award for performance, sportsmanship and team spirit.

The experience of travelling overseas and representing his country improved Dylan's outlook a lot.

Imagine how proud you would feel.

And how happy you'd be to see your family and friends are proud of you too.

After feeling bad about yourself, starting to feel proud of yourself instead is quite a turnaround.

It can give you a sense of purpose and a renewed positivity!

Dylan didn't know it then, but things were about to take off in the world of wheelchair tennis for the thirteen-year-old boy. And the inspiration came from that trip overseas representing his country.

He was determined to become more independent.

He was determined to lose weight.

This first thing he did was tell him mum he was going to push himself home from school every day. It was a long way home and it's hard for cars to see a boy in a wheelchair. His mum was worried it wasn't safe and refused – at first.

But Dylan insisted!

It was hard for him to push the three kilometres to school and then back home again carrying all his schoolbooks, but he did it. It improved his fitness and made him stronger for his tennis, as well as making him more independent.

The fitness helped him lose weight but what really helped was cutting out the junk food.

He was determined to get his weight down and he stuck to a healthy diet.

He lost an amazing 20 kilograms.

Losing that weight and increasing his independence gave him confidence.

But the feeling of isolation wasn't gone.

Not yet.

No matter how old you are, there is one thing that is very important.

Being left out by your friends can hurt more than anything.

Dylan found out that kids at school were having parties and he wasn't being invited. Even one of his best friends at school had a party and hadn't invited him.

Luckily, Dylan had a supportive family, especially his brother Zack who he was very close to.

He asked him how he would handle not being invited to a party that all his friends were going to. Zack said he'd just go anyway.

Or in his words – **JUMP THE FENCE**.

Dylan didn't jump the fence of course, but decided to go to his best friend's party even though he wasn't invited.

In his book, *Able*, Dylan describes how he mustered up the courage to turn up at the front door of his friend's house and ring the doorbell. He was very nervous.

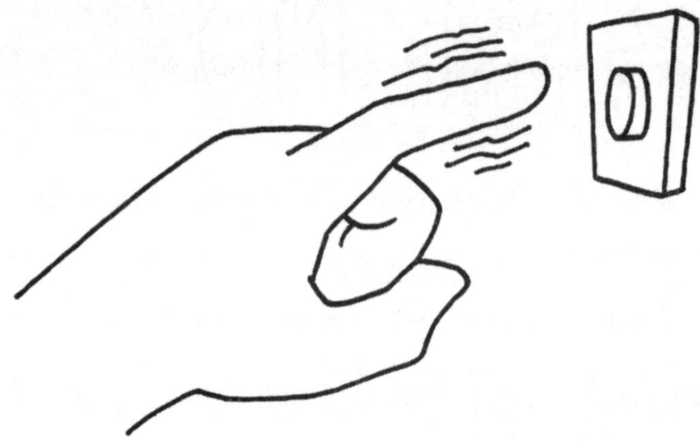

His friend opened the door.

At first it was very uncomfortable.

They both looked at each other.

But then his friend said he was sorry, and that he hadn't invited him because there were so many stairs in his house. It turned out Dylan hadn't been invited to the parties because people didn't know what his requirements were.

They'd been too embarrassed to ask about his disability.

And he'd be too embarrassed to ask why he wasn't being invited.

But finally, by being brave and confronting the issue, it was resolved. It was a lesson well learned, and it was the last stepping stone to getting over his isolation.

In wheelchair tennis, things just kept getting better and BETTER.

In 2005 and 2006 Dylan played in more junior World Team Cups, first in Groningen, Netherlands, then in Brasilia, Brazil.

By the age of sixteen, he had reached a ranking of 100 in international wheelchair tennis.

But something else was going on at that time too.

From 2004, he had been also interested in wheelchair basketball.

The Australian wheelchair basketball team is called the Rollers, and a former Roller, Shaun Groenewegen, met Dylan at a wheelchair sports open day. He suggested Dylan give basketball a try.

Shaun took him under his wing and after a few games in a local comp, Dylan started specialist training to hone his skills.

For a start, he had all the wheelchair skills he'd learned at tennis – and wheelchair mobility and pushing strength is crucial in both sports.

He had played basketball pick-up games before, with his neighbours out in the street, but this was a different level. One advantage he had was an extraordinarily long reach. His arms were longer than everyone else's – **he actually has an arm span of almost two metres!**

This meant that he could shoot pretty well, even though he was sitting in a chair.

At a junior training session, Dylan met Greg Warnecke, the coach of one of the national wheelchair basketball competition's teams –

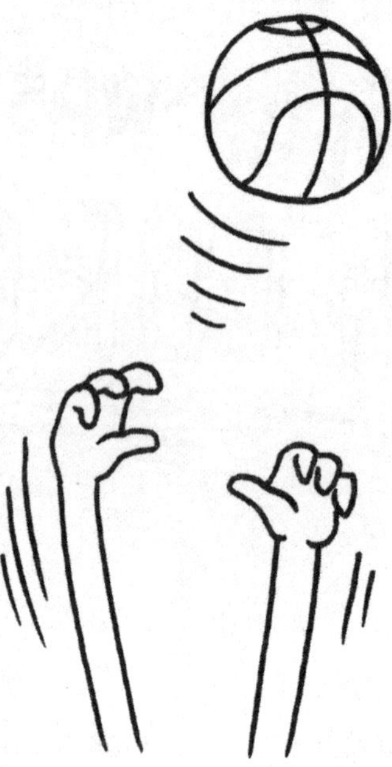

the Dandenong Rangers. Greg invited Dylan to train with the team.

One day, Dylan confided to Greg that he wanted to be a Paralympian. Greg said that he had a better chance of being a Paralympian in basketball than tennis.

That's because there's two classifications in tennis, and Dylan played in the Open classification, which meant he had to compete against players who had much greater function than he had.

But in basketball, he would be rated a "low point" player.

In basketball, there are low point players (who have a high disability) and high point players (who have less of a disability).

A team must be a mix of both. Low point players are valuable in getting a team together on the court, as they leave more room for high point players, who are usually the goal scorers and other key positions.

Dylan decided to give it crack and he continued playing with the Rangers under the keen eye of Greg Warnecke, who rated Dylan very highly. He moved from the bench to the starting five.

He was considered more valuable as time went on.

Playing with the Rangers, he was playing with and against men. But he also played with people his own age in other competitions, and actually led the Victorian junior team in two finals campaigns.

In November 2006, under Greg's guidance, Dylan was given the chance to play for Australia in wheelchair basketball, at the Far East and South Pacific Games for the Disabled in Kuala Lumpur, Malaysia.

He was still only fifteen and relatively new to the sport.

It was an incredible opportunity.

The rest of the Rollers were men, and tough men at that. He was still a boy. They didn't take it easy with him at training and the opposition didn't take it easy with him on the court.

He had to toughen up and sharpen up his game to compete with them.

He flew with the team to Malaysia to play at the 13,000-seat Malawati Stadium – the biggest venue he'd ever played at.

Imagine being fifteen, playing with men, against men, at a big stadium in a foreign country.

It would be exciting – but nerve-wracking too!

The Rollers won six matches straight.

But they fell to Iran in the final.

Even so, they won silver, and that was a pretty awesome effort for Dylan, in his first basketball international.

And the experience allowed him to dream of a chance to play in the Paralympics – less than two years away.

CHAPTER SEVEN

THE ROAD TO THE PARALYMPICS

If you're sporty and in a wheelchair, there's one place you really want to go.

The Paralympics are held “parallel to the Olympics” and are the Olympic Games for people with disabilities.

The earliest games were held at the 1948 London Olympics. World War II was just over and many people – especially military people – were left with severe injuries.

The idea came from Dr Ludwig Guttmann. He fled Nazi Germany during the war because he was Jewish, and would have faced death or imprisonment if he’d stayed. He escaped to England and was welcomed as a refugee.

Dr Guttmann started the world’s first hospital spinal care unit in his adopted town of Stoke Mandeville.

He helped thousands of people with disabilities and his ideas spread around the world. One of his ideas was that patients with paraplegia or quadriplegia should play sport to improve their outcomes. He got them out of bed and into the hospital grounds. Their rehabilitation improved, and they enjoyed life more as well.

Athletes with disabilities had participated in able-bodied sports long before Dr Guttmann came along. One was Australian James Resleure, who lost a leg in a rail car accident at age 10. He won several races as a member of the Bondi swimming club and even tried out for the US Olympic team in swimming and water polo in 1912. He set several swimming records at Cambridge University.

But they were isolated cases.

When Dr Guttmann organised the 1948 International Wheelchair Games (sometimes known as the Stoke Mandeville Games), this was the first multi-sport international competition for people with disabilities.

In the beginning, the competitors were war veterans with spinal cord injuries, but as the years went on more people were invited to participate.

In Rome in 1960, 400 athletes in wheelchairs from twenty-three countries competed. In the 1976 Games in Toronto, Canada, athletes with different disabilities were included for the first time. From 1988, the Paralympics have been held immediately after the Olympic Games, in the same city.

And while his Paralympic basketball dream came closer, he was still playing wheelchair tennis.

In May 2007, he played basketball for Australia at Manchester, England, in the Paralympic World Cup; and in July he flew to Stockholm to play wheelchair tennis for Australia in the World Team Cup.

Australia got knocked out early in the World Team Cup for tennis, but made the final in basketball, only to go down to the world number one team, Canada, also known as the Canucks. They were coached by Mike Frogley, a legendary coach who would soon become an important part of Dylan's story.

The next big event was in January 2008, the Wheelchair Basketball Good Luck Beijing tournament, held in preparation for the Beijing Paralympic Games.

Dylan had just turned seventeen, and this was the first time he'd made the starting five.

He scored 6 points as Australia beat arch rivals Canada. But Australia had to meet Canada again in the final, and unfortunately went down. Although Dylan was disappointed at losing, there were two amazing positives to come out of it.

First, the Canucks coach offered him a college scholarship in Chicago where he coached the wheelchair basketball team at the University of Illinois Urbana-Champaign.

Dylan would have to finish Year 12 first, but the chance to learn from the best and play in the US college competition was too good to refuse.

On top of that, he was named in the Beijing Paralympic team!

His dream would finally come true.

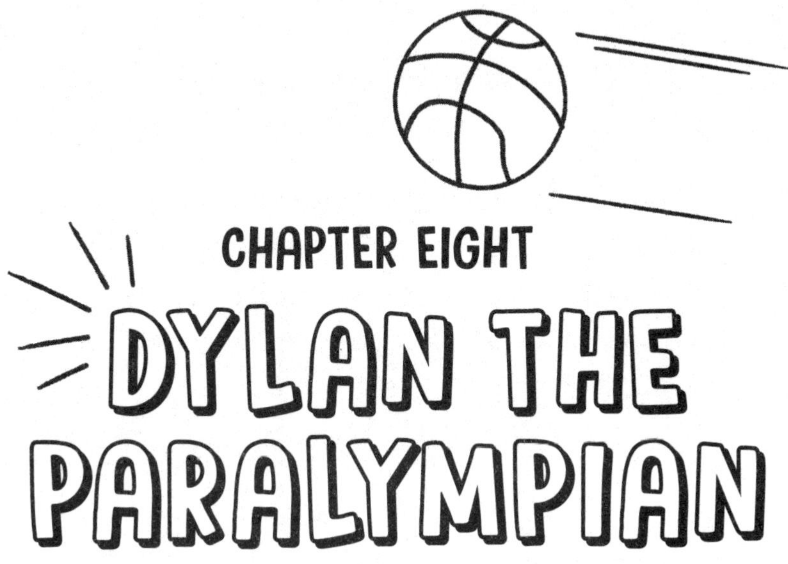

CHAPTER EIGHT
DYLAN THE PARALYMPIAN

Dr Guttman wouldn't recognise the Paralympics now!

Thousands of athletes from more than 50 countries compete and millions of fans turn up to watch the competition, hundreds of thousands of them with disabilities themselves.

At the 2008 Beijing Games for example, there were 4000 athletes and more than 3 million spectators. More than 3 billion people watched from home on TV.

Beijing is one of the biggest and busiest cities in the world. 20 million people live there!

The Paralympics was an enormous event for the city and for China. This was their chance to show their best side – spectacular stadiums, impressive athletes, facilities, well organised events.

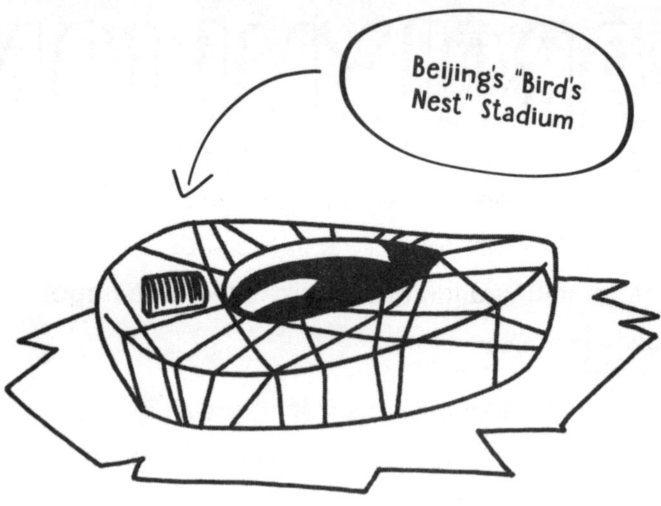

And everything was so big!

Even the food hall for the athletes was enormous. It had every type of food from around the world and the hall was so big you could hardly see the far end. It was constantly filled with thousands of people from every corner of the globe – Europe, Australia, Asia, Africa, the Americas.

So many people with disabilities. So many people in wheelchairs.

Imagine what it would be like for someone who's always been in a wheelchair. To be where having a disability is the most **USUAL** thing in the world.

In his book *Able*, Dylan describes seeing a Chinese swimmer, He Junquan, in the food hall. He had lost both arms at the shoulders after touching a live electricity cable at the age of three.

He carried his meal tray to the table in his mouth. Then he took off his shoes, and used his foot to hold the chopsticks. He ate without dropping a single grain of rice.

Most westerners have trouble using chopsticks even with their hands!

The Rollers came into the tournament as the third seed. The favourites were their archrivals, Canada, with the USA coming close behind. It was going to be hard to even make the final.

Dylan was the baby of the team – a full six years younger than the second youngest player. But he would have a part to play.

He rolled out with the Rollers into the packed National Indoor Stadium.

One of the TV commentators said Dylan looked about twelve years old. He was actually seventeen.

They won their first match in a thriller, beating **Brazil 73–72**, followed by victories over Great Britain, China and Israel, before going down to the **USA 61–68**. They shook off the loss and won the next two matches to make the final.

Despite only playing fifteen minutes each game, Dylan scored in most of the matches.

Now he was preparing for the biggest game of his life. The gold medal match at the Paralympics.

But they were up against the best in the world. Canada. Coached by the best coach, Mike Frogley, and boasting wheelchair basketball superstar Patrick Anderson who scored 32 points in their semi-final.

The Canucks had the edge over the Aussies, and everyone knew it would be an uphill battle.

The stadium was packed – 12,000 people and not a spare seat. The crowd was colourful, noisy and excited. They were calling out players names and cheering on their team to try harder, to go for gold!

THE BUZZER GOES.

Ten players wheel hard, crashing, moving from one end of the court to the other, never resting.

They circle, spin and zoom up the court and back down again. Fighting over the ball, shooting, rebounding, grappling.

The game is in constant motion. It's tiring just to watch. But it's exciting.

Very exciting!

Dylan is desperate to get on the court.

He has started on the bench. He keeps looking to the coach Ben Ettridge, hoping for the call up to play. But all first quarter, nothing happens. He's stuck on the sideline.

In the second quarter Australia is behind by three. The coach needs something different to spark a surge, and halfway through the second quarter, he puts Dylan out there.

The crowd stamps the rhythm to the Queen song *Another One Bites the Dust*.

STAMP STAMP CLAP!
STAMP STAMP CLAP!

Dylan is wearing

He rolls out, looking small amongst the bigger men, but he immediately gets stuck in, harrying the opposing players, chairs clanking together as he gets in their face, but careful not to give away a foul.

He's a terrier, always at them!

The Rollers have the ball and Dylan moves to the edge of the three point line. He gets the ball, lines up and delivers a pin-point pass to team-mate Shaun Norris who shoots for two.

Already Dylan has an assist, and the score is getting closer – only one point behind!

There is a collision, like a car crash for wheelchairs, and Shaun's chairs upends. It's not unusual – that happens a lot. Then the powerful Canadian Patrick Anderson smashes into Dylan so hard he lands on top of him!

Ouch!

It's a hard slog, and at halftime Australia is four points behind.

The Canadians are aggressive, strong and relentless. It is going to be hard to get on top of them. But the Rollers play aggressively too, attacking without fear and putting their bodies and their chairs on the line.

By the end of the third quarter, Australia is in the lead.

The final quarter is tough and the big Canadians try to roll over the Aussies.

Dylan is on the court when the final buzzer goes.

The Rollers have held on, taking out the game 72–60.

WINNERS!

The rest of the team roll onto the court and embrace each other as Waltzing Matilda belts out over the loudspeakers.

Shaun Norris hugs Dylan, just about tipping them both out of their chairs.

The Rollers are one of the great Aussie teams – and all the players are now gold medallists!

Dylan now had GOLD!

And he was only seventeen!

The youngest ever Australian to win a Paralympic basketball gold.

Dylan's family is in the crowd, cheering so much they can longer talk. They are beaming, showing how proud they are.

His dad hugs him so tightly he nearly cuts off his windpipe. They are all crying – even Zack is crying tears of joy and relief at the amazing feat his brother has just achieved.

The whole team heads to the dais, lining up across the floor in their green and gold track suits.

The national anthem plays and the medals are handed out, one by one. When Dylan gets his, he can't help but cry.

In his darkest hours, when he was made to feel worthless by bullies, he could never have dreamt he would be here. Here with a champion team.

A champion himself.

CHAPTER NINE
DISASTER STRIKES

Dylan was on top to the world.

He flew home, not even eighteen years old, and already a world champion.

He sat his Year 12 exams in the school hall, while at home he had a gold medal!

Despite spending so much time and effort on his sporting career, he still did well at school and graduated with good marks.

He also received an Order of Australia Medal, along with the rest of the team, for the incredible effort of winning gold in Beijing.

How could things get any better?

After graduating, Dylan did what many other teenagers do – he relaxed and had a great time. He went to music festivals – despite the difficulties of getting around in a wheelchair. He spent time with his girlfriend Chelsy – **YES**, teens in wheelchairs ***can*** have girlfriends!

And Dylan went all the way to the United States to play under Canada's coach Mike Frogley.

Chicago was cold.

VERY COLD!

But it was worth it. He learned so much from his new coach, and he also started his studies in commerce. His university team won the national college competition, going through undefeated.

And he learned about a different country. After the academic year ended, Dylan travelled around America with his brother Zack.

Dylan loves music and he went to lots of festivals and concerts while he was America. At one Jay Z concert he got fed up with not being able to see properly – so he invented the sport of "wheelchair crowd surfing".

He asked the crowd to pick up his chair, and they carried him towards the stage!

Jay Z saw him and gave him a shout out! He's done this many times since.

When his time in Chicago was done, Dylan came back to Australia and moved into a St Kilda apartment with his friend and training partner Jannik Blair.

He enrolled to finish his commerce degree at the University of Melbourne, and picked up work as a motivational speaker touring Victorian schools, trying to inspire the next generation of Paralympians as well as helping all kids improve their lives through sport.

On top of the Paralympic gold, the Rollers had just won the Wheelchair Basketball World Championships – the first time Australia had won the competition. Now Dylan started preparing for the London Paralympics.

Everything seemed wonderful.

BUT THEN – DISASTER STRUCK!

In March 2012, Dylan went to a function at his brother's work. It was a bit of a wild party, and someone had dropped a glass on the floor and not cleaned it up. The broken glass was near Dylan's wheelchair, but he didn't pay any attention to it.

Then a person who knew Dylan came over to say hello. This person thought it would be funny to pick Dylan up, wheelchair and all.

It wasn't funny.

Not at aLL.

Dylan fell out of the chair and landed on the broken glass. He instinctively put his right arm out to protect himself – and his hand was cut to pieces.

Blood spurted out from his wound. The floor was covered in blood and glass, and blood was shooting everywhere, even into his own face.

People were panicking and running around madly. The security staff rushed to him. One of them had a towel and wrapped it around his hand. Zack squeezed the towel hard onto the wound to stop the bleeding, while a guard wrapped gaffer tape tightly around it.

Dylan had severed an artery.

He would have bled to death right there and then if they hadn't acted quickly.

An ambulance arrived and rushed him to hospital.

It was obvious something was wrong – Dylan had a serious life-threatening wound.

But he felt it was even worse than that. He felt something very, very bad had happened to his hand.

After the doctor's cleaned up the wound and stitched it, Dylan was no longer in imminent danger.

But the surgeon asked Dylan to move his fingers.

Dylan tried.

But nothing happened!

He tried again. Still no movement!

Make a fist, the surgeon said.

Still nothing!

OH NO!

This was really, really, REALLY BAD!

If he couldn't move his fingers, he couldn't play basketball anymore.

He couldn't even push his chair! How would he get around?

Imagine how bad it would be if you found you couldn't use your right hand. That would be tough. But then imagine it for a person who couldn't use their legs either. They would only have one of their four limbs working. It would be devastating.

The doctors took scans and discovered that, on top of his artery and tendon being cut, Dylan's ulnar nerve was severed. This was serious. Very serious.

If he didn't have surgery IMMEDIATELY, he would lose the use of his hand forever.

He went into surgery straight away.

It was difficult and took a long time, and everyone was nervous about how it would turn out. Eventually it was completed.

And it was a success!

But there was three months of rehab to get his hand working. And even then, ***it would never be the same again***.

Luckily for Dylan, he was living with his friend, and even though Jannik was also in a wheelchair, he acted as Dylan's carer during his rehab. Until Dylan's hand was fully healed, he couldn't get dressed or even get out of bed by himself.

He was determined to recover as quickly as he could. He spent every minute doing his rehab, eager to get back to his independence.

But while the rest of the Rollers were preparing for the London Paralympics, he had to sit at home.

When the Rollers went to Belgium for an Olympic lead-up tournament, he couldn't go.

Was his basketball career over?

As London drew nearer, he started to wonder if he would be replaced, even if he did manage to recover.

Would the selectors remember him?

He continued to work hard on his rehab, and he and Jannik practiced daily in cold stadiums by themselves, working on their fitness, skills and speed. Getting ready for the call up.

His hand was getting better, but it would never be like it was.

Then the day came, and the Paralympic team list came out.

Jannik was on it.

And Dylan was on it!

THEY WERE
GOING TO
LONDON!

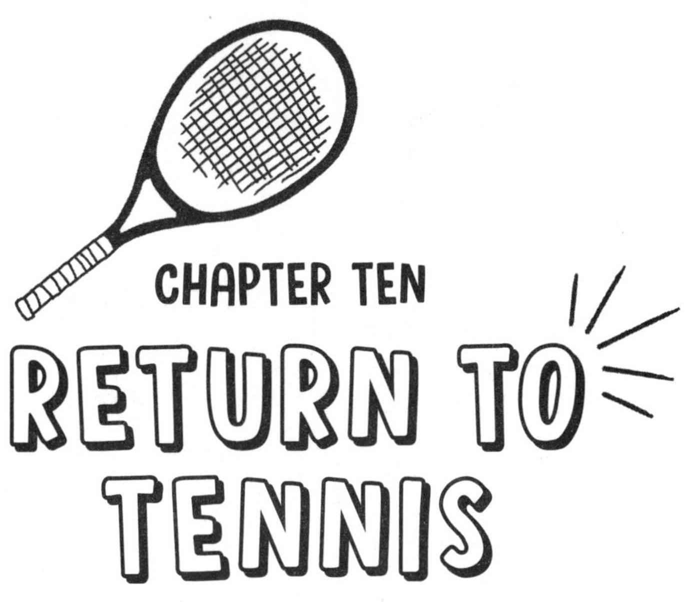

CHAPTER TEN

RETURN TO TENNIS

In August 2012 Dylan flew with the rest of the Australian contingent to London for the Paralympics.

They were the World Champions and the Paralympic champions.

That meant they had targets on their backs!

No one wants to be seen as the favourites, because then all the other teams are out to beat you.

Beat the favourites, and you know you're better than the best!

But it didn't bother the Rollers. They surged through all-comers, making it to the final against their old adversary, Canada.

It was a noisy, exciting match. Fans on both sides were going wild.

Australia led by one point at quarter time, and still led by one point at half time.

Patrick Anderson, as usual, was causing trouble for the Rollers. He was charging up the middle, spinning 360s, and seeming to score at will. He sank a basket just after the break – making his tally 17 – putting Canada in front.

The Aussies were four points behind going into the last period.

Anderson had come out of retirement to help Canada, and was compared to Michael Jordan or Kobe Bryant in the London Paralympics. The commentators were saying that like Jordan, the opposition knows exactly what he's going to do – but he's so good there's nothing they can do to stop it.

Anderson tore through Australia that day, scoring 34 points with 10 rebounds and 8 assists.

Canada won the gold medal by six points with a **64–58** victory. They had their revenge over Australia.

The Rollers, especially Dylan, were devastated.

Dylan had already achieved a lot in wheelchair basketball – more than most people could dream of – but this was to be his last game. Basketball had started to feel like a job for him, and losing that match helped him decide to try and see what else was out in the world for him.

As many young Australians do, Dylan took off and travelled the world for almost a year. He became a backpacker in a wheelchair.

It wasn't easy, but it was a blast!

He returned to Melbourne in September 2013 with a bagful of stories and a renewed spirit – and also a bit of extra luggage around his waist.

He decided to work off the excess weight with some exercise, so he picked up his tennis racquet and started playing casually again.

He found he loved it just as much as before.

But since he last played tennis, something had changed. The injury to his hand was tragic, painful, and scary. A cloudy day for sure.

But as often happens with cloudy days, there was a silver lining.

Previously he had been classified as an open player. That meant he had to play against people with much less disability than he had.

Now, because of the permanent injury to his hand, he could qualify as a quad player.

The quad classification is for athletes with additional restrictions in the playing arm.

Dylan quickly got back into playing competition tennis. Although he had lost movement and strength in his right hand, he also had new skills he'd learned from his time with the Rollers – he could manoeuvre the chair at speed and go non-stop for long periods of time.

He had loved being in the Rollers – there's something great about being in a team and all striving for the same result. Team culture can also spur you to work harder. When Dylan went solo again as a tennis player, the increased Roller work ethic stuck with him.

But it's harder in tennis too. You are on your own. You don't get subbed off if you're hurt or tired, you just keep on playing or forfeit.

IF YOU LOSE, IT'S ALL DOWN TO YOU. NO-ONE TO BLAME BUT YOURSELF.

Dylan played in a few tournaments. He performed pretty well without winning any of them. But his old record as a junior and the fact he had a gold medal, plus some decent, if not winning performances, was enough to attract the attention of the Australian Open organisers.

Only a few months after picking up his racquet again, he was granted a WILDCARD into the AUSTRALIAN OPEN!

Dylan's first game was against one of the greats of wheelchair tennis: **David Wagner**, an American who had become a quadriplegic after diving into shallow water and breaking his neck.

David Wagner
US
DyLan ALcott
AUS

The quad singles competition was usually played by the world's top four players in a round robin, followed by a final. Except this time Dylan was taking the fourth place with his wildcard.

Wagner wasn't happy about it.

To him, Dylan was a nobody who didn't deserve to be there.

He taught Dylan some lessons on the court that day. Dylan had got himself to a position to lead by one set with **THREE MATCH POINTS** up his sleeve. How can you lose from there?

But the champion held on. Wagner defended the match points, and went on to win the second set. And then he won the third set. He'd taken the match.

This was the first meeting in a rivalry that would span more than fifty matches. And it was a big lesson for Dylan.

In basketball, if you were ahead, you could slow the game down and get the win. That didn't work in tennis.

No matter how far ahead you were, you still had to hit the winning points.

Dylan didn't progress to the final.

He was sitting in a café feeling dejected when one of his idols came up to him – ***Pat Rafter. Wimbledon champion and much loved Aussie.***

Pat had seen Dylan's match against Wagner, and he and had some advice.

Dylan had to be less reactive, he said. He said you need to put the pressure on the other player, don't just sit back and wait for them to make a mistake. At this level, they might not make an error.

YOU HAVE TO TAKE THE GAME TO THEM!

Dylan listened to that advice from a great Aussie legend, and it improved his results.

He played in a number of tournaments and started doing very well. But no matter how far he progressed, it seemed he always had to meet David Wagner. And Wagner won every time, including seven straight finals.

It looked like he would never win a tournament, certainly not while Wagner was there.

Until the Belgian Open. Wagner versus Alcott in the final.

After that win, Dylan knew he could beat anyone.

Later he beat Andy Lapthorne to win the British Open in Nottingham. At the time Wimbledon didn't have wheelchair events, so he still didn't have a grand slam under his belt.

Not yet.

One year after his first attempt at the Australian Open, Dylan was back. This time it was definitely not a wildcard entry. Everyone knew he deserved to be there. He was ranked number two – but if he won the Open, it would not only be his first grand slam, he would also become the world's number one!

That's great motivation to do your best!

Dylan made it through the rounds by beating Andy Lapthorne, Lucas Sithole (who was also his doubles partner) and David Wagner.

Inevitably, he faced Wagner in the final.

This time, Dylan felt good about the match. He thought he had his measure, and was feeling fit and strong.

The crowd was more than 10,000 – big for any tennis match, enormous for wheelchair tennis. Being in Dylan's home country – and his home city – the crowd was behind him. In fact, hundreds of people in the crowd were his actual family and friends.

It was a home town crowd, no question.

They cheered loudly as Dylan wheeled onto the court. That gave Dylan a lot of confidence. There's nothing like your friends and family – your whole home town – urging you on.

Dylan was too strong for Wagner in the first set, getting an early break over his serve. And he went on with it from there, taking the set **6–2**.

The second set began the same, with Dylan racing to a **4–1** lead. The match was his – all he needed was two more games.

He had won gold in basketball, then tried to succeed at a new sport. But he kept losing the same guy, the legendary champion, sixteen years his senior.

But now, he had the upper hand.

Could he win this and become the champion himself!

Just as he was ready to take the match to Wagner, it started raining.

Play was halted.

They left the court.

With time to think, fear crept in. Dylan had led Wagner the first time they played. Then he had looked certain to win – he even had three match points up his sleeve! But Wagner came back. Wagner won that game. Dylan let it slip through his fingers.

Would that happen again?

But Dylan pushed the doubt away.

I CAN DO THIS!

I WILL DO THIS.

This is the Australian Open!

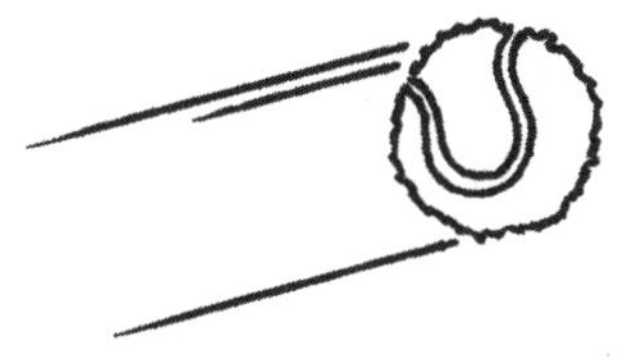

The rain stopped and they went back onto the court.

Wagner won his service game, and the score went to **4–2**.

But Dylan won his too.

5–2.

Dylan would win if he broke serve. But again, Wagner held on.

5–3.

Dylan now had the chance to serve for his first grand slam.

THE BIG ONE HE'D DREAMED OF. HIS HOME GRAND SLAM.

YOU **CAN**
DO THIS!

He concentrated, and took the game to Wagner. He didn't wait for him to lose, he pressured him into making a mistake.

And again. And again. And again!

He did it! Dylan won!

Game, Set and Match to Dylan Alcott!

CHAPTER ELEVEN

THE GOLDEN SLAM

After the Australian Open win, things **just kept getting better and better** for Dylan's tennis career.

In August 2015, Dylan followed up his hometown win by taking the US Open, again beating David Wagner in the final!

6–1

4–6

7–5

That same year he graduated from the University of Melbourne with his commerce degree – quite an achievement considering how much tennis and basketball he had been playing since he started studying.

The following year he won the Australian Open again and prepared for the big event of the year – the 2016 Paralympics in Rio de Janeiro, Brazil.

As he was preparing for the games, he renewed his friendship with Heath Davidson. Heath and Dylan had been moving in different circles for years and hadn't seen much of each other. Heath had a few difficulties over that time and had given up tennis. But he was inspired to get back into the game and contacted Dylan. They started practising together.

It was like the old days, putting in huge training sessions. They planned to be doubles partners again – this time at the Paralympics! But first, Heath had to impress the officials enough to be granted a wildcard.

They trained so hard they felt like their arms were falling off, pushing each other to go harder and harder. One time they did ***two hours of uphill sprints***, neither wanting to stop until the other did.

The intense training paid dividends. They won the doubles events in South Africa. Then they won in Japan. Then they played in the World Team Cup – and for the first time ever Australia won the quad doubles.

They had done enough to impress. They were chosen to represent Australia in the Paralympics.

As well as the quad doubles, Dylan was playing in the singles. If he won the gold in Rio, he would be among the select few people to win Olympic or Paralympic golds in multiple sports.

The list of people who had managed that included Johnny Weissmuller who won Olympic gold for the US in swimming and in water polo in the 1920s. (He later became a very popular movie star, playing Tarzan in many films, all of them showing off his powerful swimmer's physique.)

The only Australian to manage it was Teddy Flack way back in 1896, winning Olympic golds in athletics and tennis. No Australian had won Paralympic golds in two sports.

Dylan was training hard.

His training regime consisted of two and a half hours on court training in the morning, and speed and agility drills in the afternoon. Five hours, six days per week. Plus he did up to four weight training sessions per week, as well as boxing and other one-on-one sessions with his trainer Eddie Espinosa.

Dylan had quite a team helping him as well, including Tennis Australia's high performance manager Alex Jago and sports psychologist Anthony Klarica.

Anthony offered some good advice to help him avoid choking – that is when an athlete gets overwhelmed and freezes up, forgetting all their training at just the wrong time. He said to think of something that always makes him happy. Dylan had one memory that always made him happy – his childhood cat, Chad.

He told Dylan to ***think of Chad*** as a tool to clear his head and relax. It would give him a reset to get over any jitters.

At Rio, Heath and Dylan progressed all the way to final and faced American pair David Wagner (again!) and Nick Taylor.

They were getting thumped by the American pair, down one set to love and **1–4** in the second set with the game at **0–40**.

One mistake they'd lose service and lose the gold.

But they fought back, fighting hard. They came back to win that set, and then took the final tight set to win

4–6

6–4

7–5

It was incredible. Two friendless, overweight kids who had bonded when Dylan was ten years old. Now, sixteen years later they got together to win gold!

BUT DYLAN HAD ONE MORE THING TO PROVE.

He faced British champion Andy Lapthorne for the singles gold medal.

Dylan was doing well, taking the first set **6–3** and **5–4** up in the second.

But when he was serving for the match, Lapthorne fought back, saving the point and pushing the game back to deuce. Dylan won the next point to reclaim the advantage.

Now he was serving for gold. **For history.**

Nerves started to get the better of him. His arm was shaking. The pressure was so great!

He knew what he had to do.

He thought of his cat, Chad.

The image in his mind of his old friend calmed him. All at once he was relaxed.

He bounced the ball, threw it in the air and served a screamer!

ACE!

Dylan had done it. Paralympic gold in two sports! What no Australian had ever done before.

He was one of a kind.

Things continued to go even better for Dylan after that.

Following the two golds at Rio, he was named ***Australian Paralympian of the Year*** and he also won the ***Newcombe Medal for Australian Tennis Player of the Year***.

In 2017, he continued his winning ways, starting by claiming yet another Australian Open. In fact, he won it for the next five years, claiming it seven times in total. In all, Dylan won fifteen singles grand slams, and eight doubles grand slams – four of them Australian Open doubles titles with Heath Davidson.

But he still faced hard times.

In 2018, Dylan showed determination and resilience like never before. A cut on his foot had become infected, resulting in a case of cellulitis – an extremely dangerous form of bacterial infection. This was two days before he had to compete in the Australian Open.

After being on a drip in hospital and receiving serious doses of antibiotics, he made it to the court to compete. He won his first round match.

But the infection didn't go away. Still, he continued to play, having to go back to hospital for fluids and medical treatment in between matches. In the end, he won both the singles and the doubles.

Dylan continued to have success through 2019 and 2020. But 2021 was his best ever year.

He did what no male had ever done before.

A Grand Slam is winning all four grand slam tournaments in the one calendar year.

A Golden Slam is when you do that, and then also win an Olympic or Paralympic gold. Several players have done that over their careers – spread out over a dozen or so years.

But only three players have ever done it in a calendar year: Steffi Graf in 1988, and Dylan Alcott and Diede de Groot in 2021.

Dylan was only the male player to have achieved it, winning singles titles in the Australian Open, French Open, Wimbledon, US Open and the singles gold medal at the 2020 Summer Paralympics (which was delayed to 2021 because of covid).

After winning the Paralympics gold medal and sealing the calendar-year Golden Slam, Dylan announced he would not defend his medal at the 2024 Paris Paralympics. In fact, he would retire from professional tennis entirely after the January 2022 Australian Open.

He would be thirty-two when he retired.

And he had already achieved more than most sportspeople could dream of.

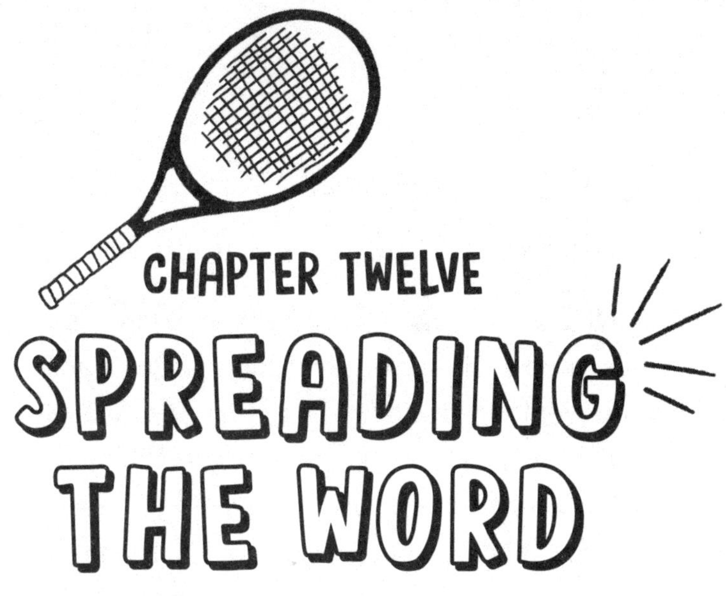

CHAPTER TWELVE
SPREADING THE WORD

On 26 January, 2022, Dylan Alcott was made **Australian of the Year**.

On 27 January, he contested the final of the Australian Open. His ***LAST*** Australian Open. He had already announced he would retire after this match.

To defend his Australian Open title on the day after Australia Day, as Australian of the Year.

What better fairytale could you possibly have?

Well, it was also his mother's birthday!

But it wasn't to be.

Dutchman Sam Schroder won in straight sets.

Nine years younger than Dylan, Schroder was seen as the next generation, a future star who would follow in Dylan's footsteps. Sam said Dylan had inspired so many people across the world, and was encouraging kids to get out and give wheelchair tennis a go. He said Dylan has had an amazing career and influenced so many people, and that Sam will try to do the same – even if it was only a small part of what Dylan has been able to achieve.

You'd think this would be a disappointment – to lose your last match in front of the world stage.

But not for Dylan.

When he was made Australian of the Year, he said that winning grand slams and gold medals wasn't his number one purpose – it was way down his list of priorities.

The reason he got out of bed in the morning was to change the way Australians see people with disabilities.

To help them realise just what a person with a disability can achieve.

So when able-bodied people see someone with a disability, they don't think about what they can't do – but all the things they ***CAN DO***.

Dylan tells a story about going into a café to buy a coffee, when a woman came up to him crying.

She told him she thought it was so inspirational to see him getting his own coffee! She assumed people with disabilities can't do anything for themselves. That it was a miracle just to get a cup of coffee!

But she couldn't have been more wrong. At the time, Dylan had won gold medals in two sports, travelled the world as a backpacker, and was a radio host on Triple J.

Dylan replied by saying that it was inspirational to see her get a coffee too!

He knew she meant well, but she had what is known as "unconscious bias". Without even thinking about it, she assumed people with disabilities couldn't do the most basic things.

That's why it's so hard for people with disabilities to get jobs, or go to big events.

The organisers don't think they can come, so they don't plan for them.

Dylan has spent his life trying to change those perceptions.

He absolutely loved music festivals. They brought such joy to his life. But he knew most promoters assumed people with disabilities wouldn't attend them, so they didn't put in ramps or spaces where they could see. **They don't plan for them**.

Dylan decided to change that by organising his own music festival – **one that includes disabled people!**

He created the Dylan Alcott Foundation to help people with disabilities, and started ***Ability Fest*** with the help of some top musicians he met at Triple J. Ability Fest is now a regular event. It has pathways for wheelchairs, accessible viewing platforms, quiet areas for people with sensory disabilities, and Auslan interpreters.

The aim – as well as giving all the people who turn up a great time – is to normalise disability.

Or as Dylan says, to ***mainstream disability***.

It also raises money to help young Australians with disabilities get sports wheelchairs – because they are very expensive compared to normal wheelchairs – and also help them get to university or start a business.

Dylan also set up **employment agencies** for people with disabilities. *Get Skilled Access* helps make businesses more accessible and inclusive, and *Recruitable* helps people with disabilities get work.

From his own experience, Dylan knows how much people with disabilities can do, and how much they can **help businesses** if they're working for them.

Dylan himself has a commerce degree and has built a multi-layered career – promoter, advocate and media star.

He has hosted *Invictus Games Today* and ABC's live music show *The Set*, he regularly commentates on the tennis on TV, and has been a radio announcer for Triple J. He won a Logie award for best TV newcomer and has a successful career as a public speaker, including making TED talk presentations.

Dylan was even the face of the ANZ bank's national media campaign – the first person with a disability to head such a campaign. He wrote his autobiography, *Able*, in 2018, letting people know about the life of someone who had been born with a disability. But it wasn't a tragedy like those old movies and TV shows when he was young.

It was about success.

ABOUT JOY.

ABOUT LIFE!

Dylan was made Australian of the Year for his efforts helping mainstream disability, rather than just his sporting career.

But he constantly uses his sporting career to promote his passion for inclusiveness.

In December 2014 he organised a 24-hour non-stop tennis marathon to create a world record and to raise awareness of the capabilities of people with disabilities. It was tremendously difficult to play for a full day without stopping, and severely taxed his body, but he played every minute of the 24 hours against other players and celebrities.

The event created a giant buzz and raised **$70,000** for charity.

Novak Djokovic is a big supporter of wheelchair tennis, and when he was raising money for a childhood education charity, Dylan hosted the event. Dylan also taught him how to play wheelchair tennis and they played a game together. The video of the event went viral and helped promote the sport globally.

For Dylan, wheelchair sport was the first place he felt included.

He says he used to hate his disability, but he learned to love it.

Being disabled enabled him to live out his dreams. He won gold medals in two sports, and has a great media career. He has also met many celebrities though his Paralympic and tennis career, including Arnold Schwarzenegger, Novak Djokovic, the Wu-Tang Clan, Will Smith, the Dalai Lama, Prince Harry, Oprah Winfrey and many more, some of whom became good friends.

He even met Queen Elizabeth II – via zoom – who laughed at his very Australian sense of humour.

There are plenty of great Australian jokes you could tell the Queen of England if you ever had the chance. Maybe next time Dylan could try this?

There's no doubt that Dylan's personal charm and charisma has helped make wheelchair tennis more popular, and now it is sometimes broadcast on the main TV channels. Channel Nine even held back the nightly news so viewers could watch his last Australian Open match live.

In early 2022, not long after he was made Australian of the Year, the Prime Minister, Scott Morrison, talked to the media about disability. He said that he was "blessed" to have children without disabilities.

One of the jobs of the Australian of the Year is to speak up FOR ALL AUSTRALIANS.

Dylan was upset about what the prime minster said. It would have been impossible for a bullied boy in a wheelchair to think that one day he would call the prime minister out.

But that's what Dylan did.

I am VERY BLESSED to wake up this morning. I reckon my parents are pretty happy about it too. Feeling sorry for us and our families doesn't help. Treating us equally and giving us the choice and control over our own lives does.

The prime minister apologised and said he didn't mean any harm, but it was another example of the unconscious bias Dylan has been fighting against.

He works tirelessly to see people with disabilities treated equally and given control over their own lives.

That's what makes him such a champion – even more than all his gold medals and world records!

THAT IS what makes DYLAN ALCOTT AMAZING!

CHAPTER THIRTEEN

WHY IS DYLAN SO GOOD?

There are plenty of skilful wheelchair basketball and quad tennis players in the world.

But what makes Dylan different? How did he get SO good?

Physically, he has a ***long reach***. That means his arms are longer than average.

When you're playing sports that don't involve your legs, that is a great advantage. In basketball it means you have a better chance to grab passes, and an advantage in shooting and passing.

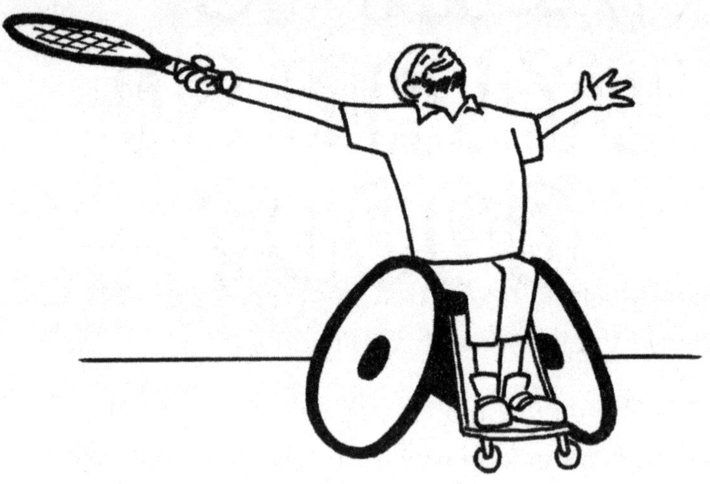

In tennis, it means you can generate more power in serves and ground shots because of your longer levers. And can also reach balls that are a little further away.

But the real advantages come from the mind and the heart.

DYLAN LOVED PLAYING!

He ***loved basketball*** and the camaraderie of being in a team. He was the youngest but he looked up to the men in the team and learned from them. And the team spirit made them all try harder for each other, improving their fitness and improving their game.

But after a while basketball started to seem like a job. Without that love of the game, you can't try your very best. So he moved on.

He went back to tennis and he remembered how much **he loved that sport**, and it drove him onto bigger and better things.

And the drive that comes from loving a sport leads to other advantages. He trained ridiculously hard. But he wouldn't have done that if he didn't love the sport.

He once trained by doing two hours of uphill sprints.

He trained five hours per day six days a week plus three or four one-on-one boxing, weight training and specialist sessions.

The more training you do, the greater strength and skill you gain, the faster you get to the ball, and harder you hit it. The more gym work he did, the stronger his upper body, enabling his powerful backhand and forehand shots and his big serve.

He has exceptional mobility. He never stops!

That came from being strong and training hard. What he learned as a junior in tennis helped him in basketball. And what he learned playing on the court with men in basketball, helped him when he returned to tennis.

Stamina is his greatest asset.

Dylan's endurance is legendary. And the more you practice your endurance, the more you can extend it. No one in the world had ever played wheelchair tennis for 24 hours straight before.

But Dylan did.

Imagine then if you have to play a match that goes longer than usual, ending up having to play for hours. For the opponent it might be exhausting.

Not for Dylan!

He Loves competing.

Losing hurts and winning drives him on. He plays through pain – even playing in one Australian Open while rushing into and out of hospital throughout the competition. **And by the way, he won the tournament**. Singles and doubles!

Tennis Australia's national high-performance wheelchair coach, Francois Vogelsberger, says Dylan has

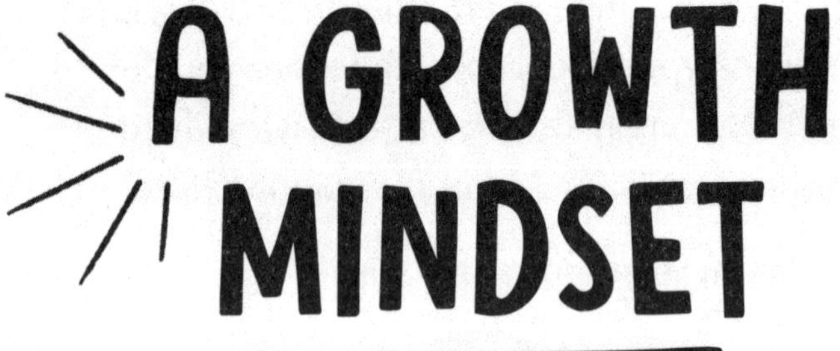

– he is always striving to be a better tennis player and a better person.

This makes him very hard to beat.

Another big weapon is his technique.

His serve has power and speed, but he can also swerve it to the left, taking it away from the opponent – and at pace.

He has a **cross-court backhand**, hitting it back across his head with the semi-western grip, which generates topspin. He uses the same grip as for a forehand, but hits the ball with the other side of the racquet – an inverted grip.

Another stroke he has developed is **the slice forehand**. Vogelsberger says his forehand was his weakness when he was younger, but he improved it over time. He keeps the ball low and adds side spin to it. It is a winning weapon.

And winning weapons are what you need at this level, as Pat Rafter told him all those years ago.

It's not good enough to sit back and wait for your opponent to make a mistake.

YOU HAVE TO TAKE THE GAME TO THEM.

Listening to advice like that and acting on it is one more thing that has made Dylan such a champion.

LEARN FROM THE CHAMPIONS WHO'VE COME BEFORE YOU.

And maybe the most important thing of all – he isn't just a tennis player or a basketball player...

Dylan has a point to prove.

He wants to show that people with disabilities are just as tough and just as entertaining as other elite athletes. He spreads the word that people should watch the Paralympics and the quad tennis and all the other sports involving people with disabilities.

And that people with a disability **CAN** do amazing things.

That dedication pushed him to the extremes of training, endurance and skill. And he has proven it, many times over.

And if you don't believe it...

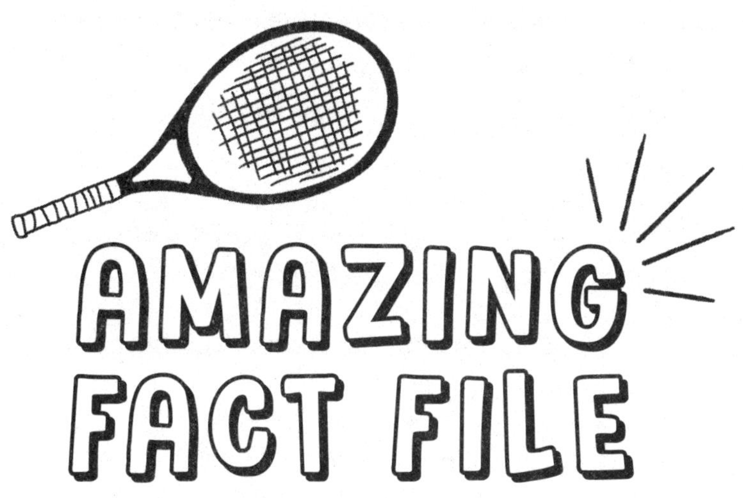

Name: Dylan Alcott

DoB: 4 December 1990

Place of Birth: Melbourne

First wheelchair tennis appearance for Australia: Junior team at World Team Cup in New Zealand January 2004, coming second but winning Team of the Year Award.

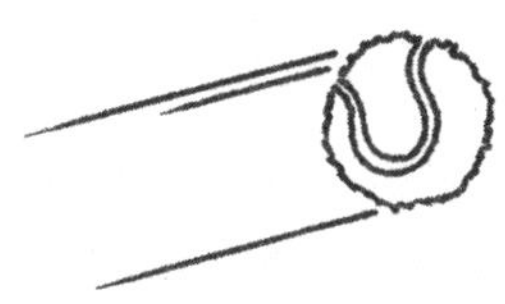

First wheelchair basketball appearance for Australia: Far East and South Pacific Games for the Disabled in Kuala Lumpur, Malaysia, winning silver, November 2006.

First quad tennis grand slam appearance: Australian Open, January 2014.

First quad tennis grand slam win: Australian Open, January 2015.

Tennis career win record: 240–54 (81.6 per cent).

Paralympic medals: Quad tennis singles Gold 2016, Gold 2021; Quad Doubles (with Heath Davidson) Gold 2016, Silver 2021. Wheelchair basketball: Gold 2008, the youngest ever Rollers Gold medal winner at 17 year of age.

Grand Slam wins: 15 singles, 8 doubles.

Australian Open: 2015, 2016, 2017, 2018, 2019, 2020, 2021. Doubles (with Heath Davidson): 2018, 2019, 2020, 2021.

French Open: 2019, 2020, 2021. Doubles (with David Wagner): 2019.

Wimbledon: 2019, 2021. Doubles (with Andrew Lapthorne): 2019.

US Open: 2015, 2018, 2021. Doubles (with Andrew Lapthorne): 2019, 2020.

Golden Slam: Australian Open, French Open, Wimbledon, US Open, Paralympics, 2021. The third person and first male in any form of tennis to win a Golden Slam in a single calendar year.

Honours: Medal of the Order of Australia (OAM) as part of the Rollers team, 2009; Australian of the Year 2022; Officer for the Order of Australia (AO) 2022.

Media Awards: Graham Kennedy Logie for Most Popular New Talent 2019.

Sports Awards: Australian Paralympian of the Year 2016, Newcombe Medal for Australia's Most Outstanding Elite Tennis Player of the Year 2016, International Tennis Federation Quad Wheelchair World Champion 2018.

Accuracy: High

Endurance: Exceptional

Special Skills: Great stamina, strong training ethic, excellent wheelchair manoeuvrability enabling constant movement, very strong upper body enabling powerful backhand and forehand shots, big serve, great slice and lob, long reach, with arm span of almost two metres.

DYLAN'S TIMELINE

December 1990: Born in Melbourne.

February 2000: Competes in Weetbix Tryathalon, aged nine.

Summer 2000: First wheelchair tennis match at a Come and Try event at the Kingsville Tennis Club in Footscray. Meets Heath Davidson.

2001: Further operations and recovery leads to total loss of movement in Dylan's legs.

2001: Offered scholarship to Brighton Grammar.

October 2001: Represents Victoria in the National Disabled Games, breaking Wheelchair Sports Australia record for the 50-metre butterfly, and winning a bronze in doubles tennis.

February 2002: Reaches the finals of the under-18 wheelchair singles tennis at the Australian Wheelchair Open aged eleven, and wins the doubles with Heath Davidson. Meets mentor Danni Di Toro.

January 2004: Australian representative debut for National Junior Team in international wheelchair competition, the World Team Cup, played in New Zealand. The team came second and won the Team of the Year Award for performance, sportsmanship and team spirit.

July 2005: Plays in the junior World Team Cup in Groningen, Netherlands.

July 2006: Plays in the junior World Team Cup in Brasilia, Brazil.

2006: Reaches ranking of 100 in international wheelchair tennis at age of sixteen.

November 2006: Australian debut in wheelchair basketball, playing in the Far East and South Pacific Games for the Disabled in Kuala Lumpur, Malaysia, winning silver.

May 2007: Competes with Rollers in wheelchair basketball in the 2007 World Cup held in Manchester, UK.

July 2007: Competes for Australia in the wheelchair tennis World Team Cup in Stockholm.

January 2008: Makes the Rollers starting team for the first time at the Good Luck Beijing tournament, a precursor to the Paralympics.

September 2008: Becomes youngest ever Australian Paralympic Gold medal winner in wheelchair basketball at the Beijing games, aged seventeen.

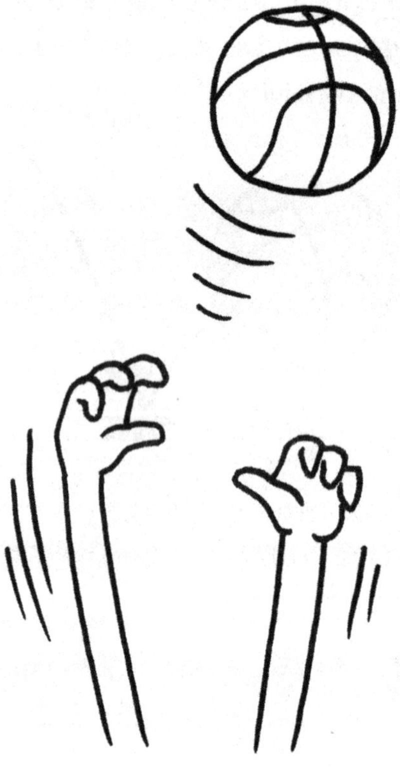

2008: Selected in All Star National League Wheelchair Basketball Team.

January 2009: Receives Order of Australia Medal, along with Rollers teammates.

September 2009: Accepts scholarship to University of Illinois Urbana-Champaign, USA, winning the college Championship Division with the university's wheelchair basketball team.

March 2010: Wins US Intercollegiate National Wheelchair Basketball competition with University of Illinois team.

July 2010: Wins Wheelchair Basketball World Championship in Birmingham UK, the first time the Rollers had ever won the championship. He was named in the All Star Team for the tournament, making him one of the best players in the world.

March 2012: Cuts hand in freak accident, severing the ulnar nerve.

September 2012: Wins silver at the 2012 London Paralympics with the Rollers, but loses in the final to Canada.

2012–2013: Backpacks around the USA and Europe.

September 2013: Returns to Australia and tries tennis again. Dylan's hand injury allows him to qualify for the quad tennis classification.

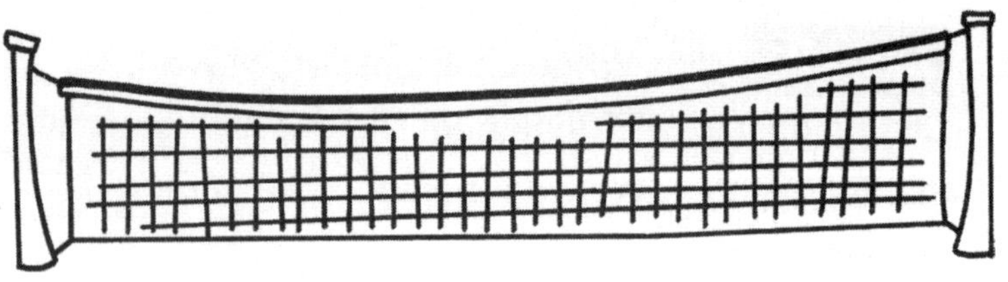

January 2014: Granted a wildcard in the Australian Open, playing against David Wagner, 16 years his senior, for the first time. Runner up in the quad doubles with Lucas Sithole.

December 2014: Completes 24-hour tennis marathon.

January 2015: Wins the Australian Open, defeating David Wagner, Dylan's first grand slam win.

March 2015: Presents TED talk at the Sydney Opera House.

August 2015: Wins the US Open.

2015: Graduates University of Melbourne with a Bachelor of Commerce.

January 2016: Wins the Australian Open.

September 2016: Wins gold medals at the Rio Paralympics in the quad singles, and in the quad doubles with Heath Davidson.

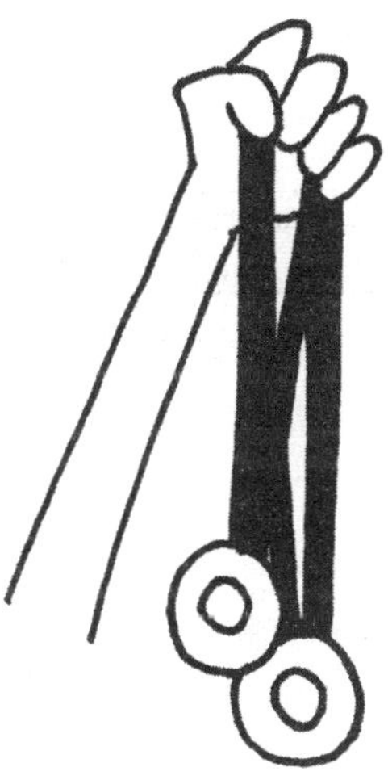

2016: Wins Australian Paralympian of the Year and Newcombe Medal for Australia's Most Outstanding Elite Tennis Player of the Year.

January 2017: Wins the Australian Open.

January 2017: Becomes the face of ANZ's national media campaign, the first person with a disability to lead such a campaign.

January 2017: Becomes a regular presenter on national radio station Triple J.

April 2017: Sets up *Get Skilled Access* and *Recruitable* agencies with Nick Morris, to help people with a disabilities get employment.

December 2017: Sets up the *Dylan Alcott Foundation* to help young Australians with a disability to achieve their potential.

January 2018: Wins the Australian Open singles championship, and the doubles with Heath Davidson, after coming straight from hospital and requiring treatment between matches.

April 2018: Runs Ability Fest in Melbourne, a music festival for people with disabilities, and a fundraiser.

2018: Writes his autobiography, *Able – Gold Medals, Grands Slams and Smashing Glass Ceilings* – with Grantlee Kieza.

August 2018: Wins the US Open.

January 2019: Wins the Australian Open singles tournament, and the doubles with Heath Davidson.

June 2019: Wins the French Open singles tournament, and the doubles with David Wagner.

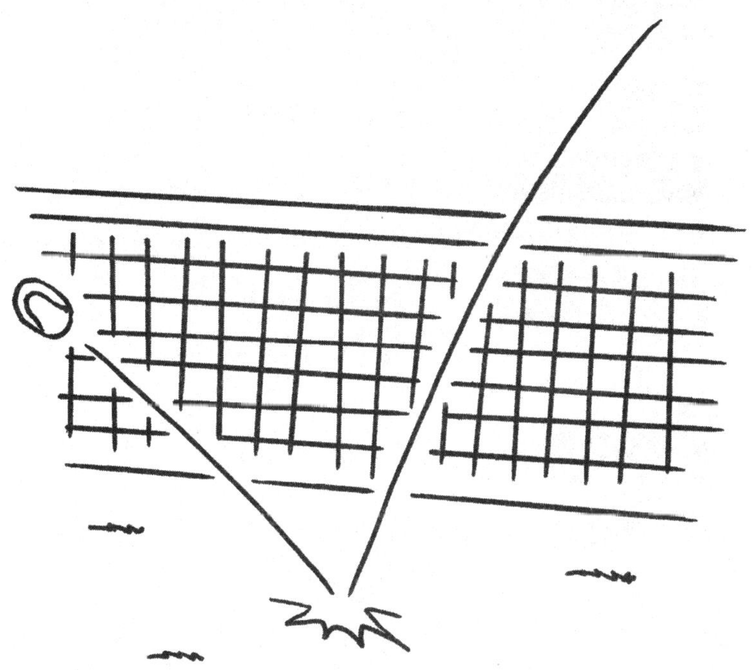

June 2019: Wins the Logie for most popular TV newcomer.

July 2019: Wins the inaugural wheelchair singles at Wimbledon, and the doubles with Andrew Lapthorne.

August 2019: Wins the US Open singles tournament, and the doubles with Andrew Lapthorne.

January 2020: Wins the Australian Open singles tournament, and the doubles with Heath Davidson.

June 2020: Wins the French Open.

August 2020: Wins the US Open doubles with Andrew Lapthorne.

January 2021: Wins the Australian Open singles tournament, and the doubles with Heath Davidson.

June 2021: Wins the French Open.

July 2021: Wins Wimbledon.

August 2021: Wins the US Open, completing a Grand Slam.

September 2021: Wins Gold in the quad singles at the Tokyo Paralympics, completing a Golden Slam – only the third person and the first male in any form of tennis to do so in a calendar year.

January 2022: Chosen as Australian of Year.

January 2022: Runner up in the Australian Open. Retires from wheelchair tennis.

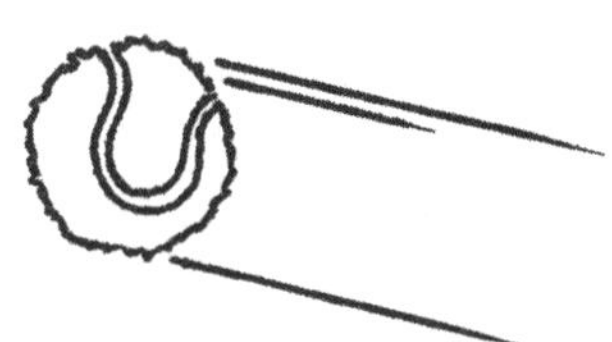

GLOSSARY OF PEOPLE

Zack Alcott: Dylan's brother who has always been a pillar of support for Dylan. A marketing and sales executive who is on the board of the *Dylan Alcott Foundation* and *Australian Festivals Association* and manages *Ability Fest*.

Patrick Anderson: Canadian wheelchair basketball superstar and widely considered to be one of the best in the world – the Michael Jordan or Kobe Bryant of the sport. Played against the Rollers and Dylan many times, notably in Australia's gold medal win in 2008, and Canada's gold medal win in 2012.

Ash Barty: Much-loved Australian tennis champion who retired at the top of her game at only twenty-five after winning the Australian Open, French Open and Wimbledon. She also succeeded in Big Bash cricket without any formal training in the sport and is a skilled amateur golfer.

Jannik Blair: One-point wheelchair basketballer for the Rollers, and Dylan's teammate, flatmate and training partner.

Heath Davidson: Friend of Dylan's and long time tennis partner. They first met in Melbourne at a *Come and Try* wheelchair tennis day when Dylan was ten and Heath was thirteen. Later, they won a Paralympic gold medal in the quad doubles, and four Australian Open quad doubles titles together.

Deidre de Groot: Dutch wheelchair tennis champion, one of only three people to complete a Golden Slam.

Danni di Toro: Australian wheelchair tennis player, 2010 French Open doubles champion and Masters double champion, and former world number one singles player. In 2015, she moved to para-table tennis and represented Australia at the 2016 Rio Paralympics, where she was team captain with Kurt Fearnley.

Novak Djokovic: Serbian champion and one of the all-time greats, with twenty-one grand slams. A big supporter of wheelchair tennis. In 2017 Dylan taught him how to play wheelchair tennis and a video of their match-up went viral.

Eddie Espinosa: A personal trainer who helped Dylan get ready for the Rio Paralympics.

Ben Ettridge: Australian wheelchair basketball coach who prepared the gold-medal winning Rollers at the 2008 and also the 2012 Paralympics.

Kurt Fearnley: Australian wheelchair racing champion. Famously crawled the Kokoda Track. He participated in the 2000, 2004, 2008, 2012 and 2016 Paralympic Games, collecting three gold, seven silver and three bronze medals.

Roger Federer: Swiss champion tennis player and one of the Big Three, with Rafael Nadal and Novak Djokovic. Has twenty grand slam titles and was world number one for 310 weeks, including 237 consecutive weeks.

Teddy Flack: Australian who won Olympic gold medals in both athletics and tennis in 1896.

Mike Frogley: Renowned Canadian wheelchair basketball coach, guiding the Canucks to supremacy in the sport. He coached Dylan at the University of Illinois, with the uni team winning the US national intercollegiate tournament.

Shaun Groenewegen: Former Roller who Dylan met at a wheelchair sport open day and suggested Dylan try wheelchair basketball.

Ludwig Guttmann: A refugee to England from Nazi Germany who established the Stoke Mandeville Games for war veterans with spinal injuries, which developed into the Paralympic Games.

Jason Harnett: Highly regarded wheelchair tennis coach who famously said players need to "think with their hands".

Alex Jago: Tennis Australia high performance manager who helped Dylan in the lead up to the Rio Paralympics.

Anthony Klarica: Sports psychologist who helped Dylan in the lead up to the Rio Paralympics and suggested he find an image in his mind to relax him if he felt he might "choke".

Dalai Lama: Spiritual leader of Tibetan Buddhism. Dylan met him by accident after ducking under a rope cordon at the 2006 World Team Cup in Brasilia.

Andy Lapthorne: British wheelchair tennis player who was Dylan's doubles partner on numerous occasions. He has thirteen grand slam titles in singles and doubles, three partnering Dylan, and is a three-time Paralympic medallist.

Jeff Minnebraker: With Brad Parks, credited as one of the founders of wheelchair tennis. Also designed the "sports car" of wheelchairs, which became the model for wheelchair sport.

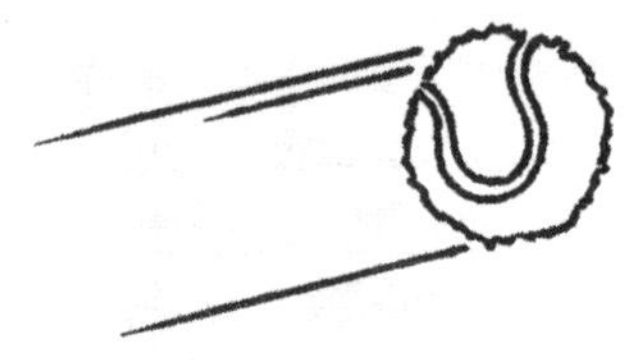

Chad Muska: American professional skateboarder, musician and entrepreneur. The Alcott brothers named their cat, Chad, after him. Thinking of Chad later helped Dylan overcome his nerves to win Paralympic gold.

Rafael Nadal: Spanish champion and current world number one tennis player with twenty-two grand slam titles and an Olympic gold medal.

Brad Ness: Mainstay of the Rollers, a five-time Paralympian and one of the greats of wheelchair basketball.

John Newcombe: Legendary Australian tennis player, one of the few men to have attained a world number one ranking in both singles and doubles. Won seven slam singles titles, a former record seventeen men's doubles titles, and two mixed doubles titles. Also contributed to five Davis Cup titles for Australia during the golden Davis Cup period.

Shaun Norris: Three-point shooting guard and key player for the Rollers. Part of the 2008 gold medal team.

Brad Parks: American sportsman credited as one of the major figures in the establishment of wheelchair tennis, together with Jeff Minnebraker.

Pat Rafter: Australian champion tennis player and former number one who won the US Open in 1997 and 2001. Reached semi-finals or better in every slam tournament in both singles and doubles.

Louise Sauvage: Renowned champion paralympic wheelchair racer who won nine gold and four silver medals at four Paralympic Games and eleven gold and two silver medals at three World Championships, as well as four Boston Marathons. Australian Female Athlete of the Year in 1999, and International Female Wheelchair Athlete of the Year in 1999 and 2000.

Sam Schroder: Dutch quad wheelchair tennis player currently with a career high ranking of number two. Has two slam titles, both won by defeating Dylan, including in Dylan's last ever match at the 2022 Australian Open.

Arnold Schwarzenegger: Giant Hollywood movie star. When he met Dylan, he delivered a line from one of Dylan's favourite movies, *Predator*, referencing a character called Dylan.

Lucas Sithole: South African quad tennis player, winning the 2013 US Open and the 2016 Australian Open doubles partnering David Wagner. Partnered with Dylan on occasion including the inaugural Wimbledon quad doubles event.

Will Smith: American rapper, and movie and TV star who met Dylan at a tennis match and later struck up a friendship, playing wheelchair tennis with him for exercise and fun.

Randy Snow: The first Paralympian to be inducted into the US Olympic Hall of Fame and the first Paralympian to win medals in three different sports: track, basketball and tennis.

Francois Vogelsberger: Tennis Australia's national high-performance wheelchair coach who worked with Dylan for seven years.

David Wagner: American wheelchair quad tennis legend. Has ten singles grand slam titles and eight Paralympic medals including three gold. Had a long running rivalry with Dylan.

Greg Warnecke: Coach of the Dandenong Rangers in the national wheelchair basketball competition. Had a great influence on Dylan's basketball career.

Serena and Venus Williams: Champion sisters who have both been ranked number one. Serena has twenty-three grand slam singles titles and Venus has seven; together they have fourteen doubles titles.

Oprah Winfrey: American TV megastar who met Dylan when she toured Australia.

Todd Woodbridge: Australian tennis player and commentator and one of the most successful doubles players of all time, winning sixteen grand slams with Mark Woodforde, together known as the Woodies.

Stella Young: Australian comedian, journalist and disability rights activist. One of the first readily identifiable Australian personalities in a wheelchair.

Able-bodied: A person or player without significant disability.

Assist: To provide the ball to the eventual scorer.

Auslan: Australian sign language

Backhand shot: In able-bodied tennis, reaching across the body to return the tennis ball with the back of the racket. Sometimes two hands can be used to grip the racquet. In wheelchair tennis the same shot is sometimes played with the front of the racquet held above the head.

Baseline: The back line of the tennis court. When serving you must remain behind the baseline, otherwise you get a foot fault in able-bodied tennis, or a wheel-fault in wheelchair tennis.

Break point: Your opponent is serving, and you are only one point away from winning the game.

Camber: The angles made by the wheels of a vehicle or wheelchair. Specifically, the angle between the vertical axis of a wheel and the vertical axis of the vehicle or chair when viewed from the front or rear. If the bottom of the wheel is farther out than the top it is called negative camber. Sports wheelchairs have greater negative camber than standard wheelchairs.

Canucks: Nickname for the Canadian wheelchair basketball team – one of the most successful of all time, the only team to have won three Paralympic titles.

Cellulitis: A deep infection of the skin caused by bacteria, usually affecting the arms and legs.

Choking: Losing by getting nerves when the win is there for the taking.

Core muscles: The group of muscles around the abdomen and lower torso. Strong core muscles help with wheelchair manoeuvrability. Dylan has less control of his core, meaning he was rated as a one-pointer in wheelchair basketball. He compensated by strengthening his upper body.

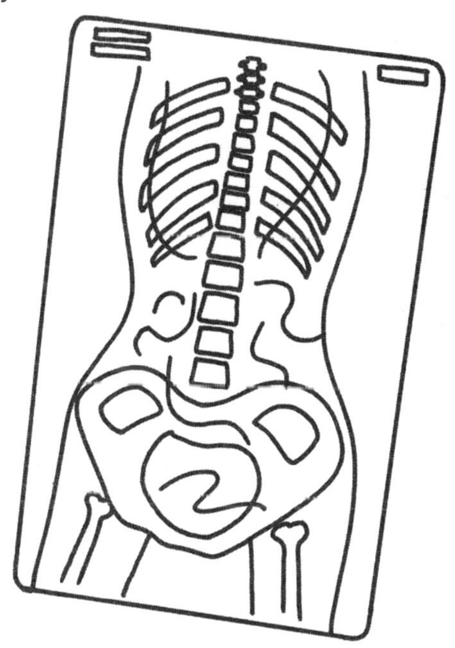

Davis Cup: The world cup of men's tennis, where teams from around the world compete. The US (32 titles) and Australia (28 titles) are the leading title holders. The Federation Cup is the women's version, recently renamed to the Billie Jean King Cup.

Deuce: When scores in a game are at 40-all it is called deuce. The first player to win two points in a row wins the game. When they win one point it is called their advantage.

Disability: In sport, physical (and sometimes intellectual) restrictions on movement, senses and activities.

Forehand shot: Returning the tennis ball with the front of the racquet by extending your arm outwards from your body.

Grand slam: The major tennis championships, the Australian Open, French Open, Wimbledon and the US Open. When all are won in a single year it called winning a Grand Slam.

Golden Slam: Winning the four majors and also the Olympic or Paralympic gold medal.

Hand rims: The outer wheels on a wheelchair. Are used to propel the chair so the rider doesn't have to touch the tyre. The rims in wheelchair tennis are sometimes made of rubber for better grip when rolling with the racquet hand.

High point player: In wheelchair basketball, a player with normal torso movement and few problems with side-to-side movement. The highest classification is a 4.5 point player. They are usually the playmakers and goal scorers.

Low point player: In wheelchair basketball, player with significant loss of torso control. The lowest classification is a one-point player, such as Dylan. They are important team players but not usually playmakers.

Mainstreaming disability: Making disability automatically accepted and included in mainstream society. An antidote to unconscious bias.

Match point: A player is only one point away from winning the match.

Paralympics: An international multi-sport event for people with physical disabilities. There are both summer and winter games.

Paraplegia: A type of paralysis that affects the ability to move the lower half of your body.

Physiotherapy: Physical therapy for injured or impaired people to help achieve better movement and health.

Quad tennis: For players who have substantial loss of function in at least one upper limb as well as the lower limbs, but may include various disabilities besides quadriplegia.

Quadriplegia: A type of paralysis from the neck down, including the trunk, legs and arms. The condition is typically caused by an injury to the spinal cord.

Rehabilitation: A slow step-by-step process to help people recover from serious injury or other ailment, so they can lead as active a life as possible.

Round robin: A competition in which every participant plays every other participant.

Seed: Ranking for a tournament. The number one seed is the player most likely to win.

Semi-western grip: A versatile tennis racquet grip enabling backhand shots with topspin.

Service game: A game in which you are serving. If the opponent beats you, they are said to have broken service.

Set point: A player is only one point away from winning the set.

Spinal cord: Transmits nerve signals from the brain to the body. If injured, the person's movement can be impeded. The degree of limitation depends on how high up the spine the injury occurred and how severe it is.

Three-point line: In basketball, the arced line 6.75 metres from the basket. Scoring outside the line is worth three points instead of the usual two.

Three-sixty: To spin completely around in a circle, as in 360 degrees.

Tie-breaker: If a set is tied at 6-6, a tiebreaker is generally played. The tiebreak continues until someone is ahead by two points and has won at least seven tie-break points.

Trunk: The body not including neck, head, arms and legs. Also called the torso.